SECOND CHANCE SUMMER

DIANA DERICCI

Purple Sword Publications
Tucson, AZ

SECOND CHANCE SUMMER
Copyright © 2015 DIANA DERICCI
ISBN 978-1-61292-144-0
ISBN 10: 1612921442
Cover Art Designed by Anastasia Rabiyah
Image Copyright Dan Skinner
Edited by Traci Markou

Published by Purple Sword Publications, LLC
Tucson, Arizona, USA
www.PurpleSword.com

The Jasper Series
Reading List:

Tougher to Love
Second Chance Summer
Finding Home
Finding Family

Chapter One

Brice Reynolds leaned over a bent and braced knee on his chair as he gathered his teaching agenda and things to take home for the weekend. A stack of tests to grade, a thousand and one things to do. At least there were only six more weeks left. He stretched, scooping the last into a sort of acceptable pile in front of him.

The light clearing of a throat drew his attention to his open classroom doorway. He smiled seeing who it was. "Hi, Terra. How was your chemistry test?"

"A nightmare," she groused. "But I know I passed."

"That's the important thing. Did you pass well?"

She crossed her eyes. "The jury is still out."

He smiled for her. "What can I do for you?"

"Uncle Ian wanted me to see if you were still on for tomorrow."

"Are you kidding? I'll be there." He let his foot drop to the floor. "Did he want me to bring anything?"

"Nope. I think Uncle Jake and Uncle Jessie have it covered. And you know when they come, there's too much of everything."

Brice smiled. Yeah, he was very familiar with the Drew family's need to stuff everyone stupid at a barbecue. "Just have him call me if he needs anything last minute. I'll be by around three otherwise."

She nodded with a smile. "See you." Clutching her backpack in her hand where it poised on her shoulder, she spun and vanished.

In the two years since moving to Jasper, he'd found the town very hospitable. He'd made several good friends, which helped life go by. One of them was Terra's uncle, Ian. They'd met at Terra's registration the fall of the previous school year. Quiet and hardworking, he owned one of the auto repair shops in town. He was also partnered with one of the local sheriffs, Caleb Drew. Well, now married. They'd done the deed over Christmas a year and a half ago. It had been a very enjoyable and intimate experience to share with them and he was thankful to call them friends.

His hands slowed closing his briefcase. Because of Ian, he'd had the chance to make new friends and meet Caleb's family, who'd all taken him in as if he'd always been there. At home, in West Virginia, he'd suffered familial obligation to be included but there was no one who embraced diversity like Ian's family did. He smirked then straightened, sliding the chair under his desk and checking that all the drawers were locked.

He couldn't say his family had truly been understanding, but what did it matter? He didn't live near them any longer. Jasper was small town America. It was friendly, and except for a few sour grapes, a pleasant community and area.

Brice had been invited to the guys' wedding, several barbecues and even a holiday gathering this last season to celebrate their anniversary. He *was* one of the family. Ian's, Caleb's and Terra's. It wasn't a bad family to have.

Arriving at Ian and Caleb's the following sun-filled afternoon, he was greeted by the scents of wood smoke. His mouth watered almost immediately. One thing he'd learned: Ian knew a mean trick or two with hot fire and beef. He stepped toward the back of the home, hearing conversation as he got closer.

A loud squeal was all the warning he got before a young brunette he recognized came tearing around the corner. He jumped out of the way. And waited. Flushed against the house, two more raced past him, laughing maniacally. Cautiously he put a foot out and when no one else appeared, he scooted around the corner, discovering several sets of eyes pinned in his direction.

He popped a thumb to gesture over his shoulder.

"Water guns," Jessie explained.

"Let me guess. She wasn't given one."

"Not yet." Jessie laughed. "Don't worry. She will get even." Jessie approached and offered a hand. "Good to see you, Brice."

"Thanks for inviting me."

A waved hand drew him deeper into the backyard. Hugs and handshakes welcomed him. Bethany, Jessie's wife, handed him a beer then tossed a filled water gun to Becky. With a war cry that would have chilled the most hardened battle soul, she charged her male cousins, Terra at her side. The battle was on now that it was even. Brice quickly found himself caught up in conversation with Ian and Caleb, laughing at their antics.

They chased each other back and forth, around the house, squirting streams of water until damp turned into soaked. At least with the warming weather and bright sunlight, they'd never feel the water chill. Summer was coming. Every single one of those kids was ready for it.

Brice barely paid the sound of a car door closing any attention, assuming it was a neighbor. That assumption soon proved to be very erroneous.

Brice spotted Jake, Caleb's youngest brother, clearing the corner of the house about three seconds before the shrillest scream of surprise silenced everyone. Maybe even those across town.

"Aaron!" Terra shoved her gun at Becky and launched for Aaron when he appeared behind Jake, jumping into him and clinging like a monkey. Luckily he caught her and held her as they kissed.

"All right you two!" Jessie scolded after about a minute, though without any real displeasure. Slowly, very slowly, Aaron let Terra reach her feet in front of him.

"So I guess that means they're still going strong, even with him in college this year?" Brice nudged Ian with an elbow.

"Still going strong." He hadn't moved too far from the grill since he'd started cooking, keeping an eye on the food he was making, glancing up every few seconds to follow Aaron and Terra holding hands to talk while a ceasefire was called in their water war. "He's a good kid, and she's no one's fool."

"They have a very supportive family. It helps."

Ian grinned and shrugged. "It doesn't hurt that the last thing Aaron wants to do is piss off Uncle Caleb, because he will tell Jessie and the hammer will come down."

Brice sniggered. He could absolutely believe that. "Did he drive?"

"Jake went to get him at the airport. It's why he wasn't here."

Brice wasn't going to confirm the fact that he'd noticed Jake hadn't been there when he'd first arrived. It really wasn't his business. He didn't want anyone else to think he was interested in Jake for more than family. It really sucked having an entire *family* of good looking men, Ian included, but Brice wasn't going to jeopardize his relationship with them by letting on that he thought Jake was gorgeous.

Since Ian and Caleb's wedding and meeting Caleb's brother who had dressed in a sharp suit for the event, Brice had harbored a bit of a crush for the other man. More than a crush since he'd allowed himself to dream. Yet a crush was all it would ever be. The man was a divorced single father, and had never once made any type of hint that he could be into men. Sometimes it happened. A man discovering he was either gay or bi after a lifetime of disappointment, or worse—failure, but among the testosterone of the Drew brothers?

Ian had already nabbed the Drew brother that played on his team. And Caleb was so completely Ian's, there was no contest.

Brice did know Jake had been single for several years, the ex having taken up with someone else and then moved out, leaving him with his daughter, a house, and a mess to clean up. He hadn't ever seen it, but he was sure the man dated. Jake might even have a girlfriend. Just because there wasn't someone there with them now meant very little.

He wasn't as broad as either Caleb or Jessie. Jessie was built like a football linebacker, and Caleb was thick. Brice didn't know for sure, but he thought there were a few years between Jake and Caleb, which put him about five years older than Brice. Not a big deal for him there, either. Brownish/black hair with the amazing blue eyes all three of the brothers had been blessed with, and a smile that could melt glaciers. He swallowed the sigh.

Yeah, Brice was totally crushing on the youngest Drew.

"Hey! Any spare hands back there?" a woman's shout came from the front of the house.

A few quick looks to see who was available, or had heard proved not many had over the kids' volume. "I'll go," Brice offered, setting his beer on one of the tablecloth-covered picnic tables as he sauntered past. He smiled when Wanda spotted him. He offered a hug in greeting and got a healthy one in return. "How's my favorite cake divas?"

"Ask mama herself."

Brice peeked over Wanda's shoulder and spotted Jeannie. "Wow! Did you swallow a soccer ball?"

Jeannie smirked, then relaxed and laughed. "Feels like it sometimes. Maybe the whole Brazilian soccer team! Rata-tat-tat."

"Or maybe the Rockettes?"

Jake's voice surprised him and he spun halfway, meeting blue eyes.

"Girl or boy, they're throwing a party. They must have got today's invitation too." Jeannie rubbed her very round tummy. "Come on, folks. This horse ain't as young as she once was."

"Quit." Wanda rolled her eyes. "She's pregnant and suddenly she's as old as time."

Brice knew better than to laugh out loud, especially in Jeannie's presence.

"Waddle yourself to the back of the house," Wanda instructed, waving to indicate *which* direction that would be. How women could manage sarcasm with hand movements alone astounded him. "I'll get the guys to help with the cake."

"Why a cake?" Brice asked.

"Special request," Wanda said. "And it's delish. Iced it this morning."

"Can't wait," Jake agreed. "It's the best part about Caleb's parties. He invites you girls." He smacked a quick kiss on Wanda's cheek before half disappearing into their SUV to pull out a large cake box. "There's two. Want both?"

"Yes, please," she replied.

"Go ahead. I'll get the other one." Brice moved out of the way to let Jake slip past after getting an eyeful of jean covered roundness, a deliciousness of his own preference, wishing more than he should have that they'd been close enough for Jake to brush into him. He didn't.

Steadying the remaining box, he waited for Wanda to close the vehicle then walked with her to the house.

"Put it in the kitchen," Caleb called. "Don't want the icing to melt in the sunlight."

Brice obeyed, following behind Jake as Wanda held the door for them. "Just leave them on the dining table. I'll get it all together when it's time for our sugar high," she told them.

Brice smiled. He really did like those two.

The door closed quietly behind the two men, Brice following Jake into the kitchen.

"There." Brice eased his box onto the table after Jake. When he turned to join the others outside, he accidentally bumped into Jake and stumbled. "Oh!" He gasped. A warm hand gathered his hip when he teetered.

"You okay?"

"Yeah. Sorry." He managed to get gravity to work for him.

The kind touch of Jake's hand vanished. "No problem. My fault."

Brice straightened his glasses and noticed Jake watching him. If he hadn't been before, Brice was blushing now. He glanced away, trying to capture his runaway libido and more graphic thoughts. "What do you think the special occasion is?"

"Who knows?"

Jake hadn't moved, still watching Brice. He couldn't control the trip of his heart being that close to his crush.

"They didn't say?"

"Nope. Might just be a because cake."

"Two layers?" *Oh God! Stop! You're sounding asinine.* Not that yelling at himself seemed to really help. This was the first time Brice had spoken more than few words to Jake and he couldn't seem to stop himself. Hearing the sound of his voice... He could listen to that deep voice read *The Decline and Fall of the Roman Empire*, in full.

Jake gave him a crooked grin and shrugged.

Feeling worse than a fool, he determinedly gathered his weakened control and followed a few paces behind when Jake left the kitchen.

Chapter Two

Jake sat at one of the tables, next to his daughter and his sister-in-law. He wrapped a hand around his beer and slowly sipped, absently listening to the two of them talk.

"Hey, Dad?"

"Hmm?" He tried to focus, his daughter's insistence finally drawing his attention.

"Aunt Bethany says maybe I should see if I can talk to someone who has a garden, to help me get a better grade on my agriculture paper."

"That's actually not a bad idea." He rested his chin on a propped fist. "What were you thinking?"

"Well." Rebecca's brow tightened. "I was thinking I could use a gardener's viewpoint versus the bulk production as one point."

"True. You could also compare issues and solutions. See if small farming or home gardening has the same kind of problems agribusiness has."

"Oh! That's a good one!" She beamed.

"I just don't know anyone with a garden," Bethany said, then she smirked. "I kill houseplants. I'm not someone to ask."

Jake chuckled and even Becky laughed. Bethany was good at a lot of things. Having a green thumb wasn't one of them, and that was a well-known family fact.

"Ask Uncle Caleb. Maybe he or Ian knows someone," Bethany offered.

"But they live here," she argued.

"And you have email and a phone. I'm sure you can figure out a way to work with such archaic technologies." Jake arched an eyebrow at her.

"There's always pen and paper and that even less-known artifact, the postage stamp."

"Oh, burn," Jake teased, laughing as Rebecca rolled her eyes at him.

She huffed. "Fine. I'll ask."

"Hey, it's just a huge chunk of your final grade. Not like you really wanted to go to Stanford or anything." He waved his bottle in mocking dismissal.

"Okay! Okay, I get it. Sheesh." She popped up and left the two adults at the table, all but stomping off.

"Well played," Bethany said, offering a palm to high five. Jake quietly returned it.

"Were we really that bad for our own parents?" He watched his daughter pout for a few minutes. It wouldn't last.

"In spades," she admitted. She glanced to the side. "Oh, Ian's waving. I guess the good stuff is ready. Time to bring out the cold."

"Need some help?"

"I'll never turn down an extra set of hands."

Swallowing the last of his beer and setting the bottle down, he trailed Bethany into the kitchen to bring out the refrigerated food.

A couple of trips brought potato salad, cold pasta salad, beans, tinfoil-wrapped corn on the cob, condiments and all the necessary things to eat it with. All the kids sat together, Terra almost on Aaron's lap. He shook his head. He hoped Ian was watching them. It didn't make an ounce of difference that Aaron was his own nephew, he didn't trust hormones. That was personal experience.

Just as he was about to sit down, he realized the last spot open was next to Brice. He hunted, but unless he wanted to eat with the teenagers... He placed his laden plate down on the almost crowded tabletop. "Any last requests?" He glanced at faces surrounding the table. Yeah, he was stalling. When a round of headshakes didn't give him an out, he sat beside the history teacher.

Correction: *cute* history teacher.

Especially when he played with his glasses. And he was stumped realizing that little tidbit. Spiky blond hair and the brightest, greenest eyes Jake had ever seen on a person. Today wasn't the first time they'd bumped together at gatherings. Brice was a close friend of Ian and Caleb's. He'd even been at their wedding.

Today was the first time, however, they'd managed to be close enough for Jake to see right into his eyes, to spot the faint freckles across his nose, and to hear the drawled cadence in his voice. It wasn't there usually and hearing it when they'd bumped into each other had surprised him.

Those few seconds suspended in time was also when Jake had realized the man was cute.

He bit at his lip, stuffing his mouth to not speak unless he had to. It was a startling fact. *Attraction.* Something that had happened infrequently through the years of his own marriage and not really since his disaster of a divorce. He hadn't given it any real thought since school. He'd been married for heaven's sakes! Jake had never gone beyond exploring with another guy. Yes, he'd played a little in college, and it all ended when Sissy had become pregnant. Jake still wasn't sure how the condom failed, but Rebecca was undoubtedly his, even down to her facial expressions.

He'd never gone as far as having sex with a guy, mostly hot make-out sessions, and few enough of those that he could count them on one hand. He wasn't going to deny he'd thought some guys were absolutely worth staring at. But that was then. Before Sissy. When he was young. Then he'd have been more open to the possibility. Now? He just didn't know what to think.

Wasn't he too old now? Wasn't he past the infatuation stage? He hadn't really thought it was even possible now. It hadn't crossed his mind. Jake had Rebecca to raise. How could he be looking at a guy at his age? ...a man? Shouldn't he be feeling this kind of...whatever...around women? He just didn't know. His thoughts tumbled hard.

"Starving Jake?" Caleb ribbed from across the table.

"Huh?" He blinked to take in his brother's smirking face. He glanced down and realized he'd chowed down through almost everything, including the plate. He swallowed. "Yeah, I guess I was. It's all so good."

Ian snorted. "You say that every time I barbecue."

"No!" he said, probably way too exuberantly by the slight jump of the body next to him. He racked his brain for a suitable framework of words, also known as a sentence. "You should do the July Fourth cook-off. This is good enough to win, easily."

"Finally!" Caleb motioned to Jake in approval and agreement. "I've been telling him that since last year. He won't believe me."

"It's just brisket and chicken."

"And what are the three things most of them cook?" Caleb asked, leaning into Ian's shoulder to egg him on.

"Brisket, ribs, and chicken," Bethany offered.

"Exactly! I know he could wipe the floor with what he makes." Caleb was beaming with pride for his husband.

"There are some experienced guys who do those cook-offs," Ian argued. "So I know how to light a fire." He licked his fingers then wiped them on a paper towel from the roll in the middle of the table, already dismissing the possibility.

"No. I think Caleb is right." Brice cleared his throat, glancing down the opposing side bench at Ian then around the table. "Since I didn't know anyone in the competition, I offered to be an alternate judge last year, and then was scared spitless when they called on me. This beats the shit out of what was boxed last year."

Jake had to take a second look. He never would have expected the teacher to cuss.

"I'd have to agree with him," Jeannie added. "I had some of last year's meat plates and none of them were this good." She petted her stomach in round circles.

Ian was starting to pinch his lips in denial.

"What would be so bad about trying?" Brice asked. "We'd help." He glanced around until he got several head nods.

"Like be my team?" Ian straightened, rising off his elbows to maybe—*maybe*—pay attention.

"Well, of course we would," Wanda jumped in.

"And I'll make the sides again so you can do the sales like everyone else."

"You guys are serious? You really think it's that good?" Ian gaped at them all.

"Hold on." Jessie stood enough to twist to address the next table. "Hey kids. Uncle Ian is going to enter the cook-off. What do all of you think?"

A loud barrage of hoots, hollers and cheers instantly filled the summer afternoon.

"You can't fool a teenaged stomach," Jeannie said, laughing behind her hand.

"My case is made." A smug Jessie sat again.

"I don't know one thing about how to do it," Ian tried.

"Um, you start the fire," Jake drily intoned repeating Ian's own words, grinning when Brice snickered at his side. He batted away the crumpled paper towel tossed in his direction.

"Okay. I'll do it." Ian gave them a firm glare. "But I'm not a one man army here. I will need help."

Brice, Jake, Bethany, Wanda and Caleb all raised their hands.

"Awesome," Brice breathed as conversation started up briskly about preparing for the cook-off and getting Ian entered. "This is going to be a good summer."

Jake tilted to stare at the man's profile. "That's right, you're almost out of jail for the summer."

Brice sipped on a tumbler of iced tea, then said, "Six more weeks."

The open collar of Brice's polo-style shirt gaped when he moved on his seat, giving glimpses of pale skin and muscle.

An arm reaching in between of both broke his frozen staring.

Ian was tossing plates into a trash bag. "Time for dessert."

Jake released a slow breath, glad for the interruption. No telling how long he would have been doing that, or if Brice would have noticed.

Wanda clapped. "Sweet! Let me go get it ready." Jeannie smiled and let her go.

"What's the big occasion?" Jake asked.

Jeannie's eyes twinkled. "You'll see."

Ian carried the now double-decker chocolate iced cake, and placed it on the adult's table.

"Now we can tell." Wanda was waving Jeannie over to her, with Ian and Caleb drawing up on her other side.

The kids were inching closer, the pull of high-dose sugar seductive.

"What?" Brice asked.

Caleb stood next to Ian in front of the crowd of family around them. Jeannie finally clasped hands with Wanda, her loose hand protective on her stomach while standing beside Caleb.

"Well, we've talked to Ian and Caleb a lot since we've become friends, and when we lost the first IVF, they were there for us. And trust me, you've never seen anything more pathetic than two lesbians crying together." Wanda grinned, teasing as she softly kissed her wife's cheek as her joke received chuckles. "The doctor put Jeannie on a regimen that was in a word: evil. But she's a trooper and we have our little angel—"

"Soccer player," Jeannie interrupted under her breath.

"—to prove it. So we have two announcements to make. One is we are having a little girl." Cheers and whoops rose up quickly and loudly. She lifted a hand and dropped it for silence. "The second announcement is Caleb and Ian have agreed to be our baby's godparents."

"That's wonderful!"

"Awesome!"

"Congratulations!"

"Wow! Godparents," Jake said. "Congrats, bro." He hugged Caleb. "You sure you don't want one of your own? I have one, she's almost fully housebroken—"

Caleb laughed, cuffing Jake on the shoulder. "Nah. She's already learned all your bad habits."

"Considering the job you're doing with Terra, I have high hopes for you two being good for ours," Jeannie said, a hint of mischief in her tone. "I mean, really. She'll be able to change her own tires and oil, *and* shoot a bull's eye from fifty yards."

Ian laughed. "Uh huh. And learn poker. There must be balance," he added piously.

"Did someone say poker?" Terra piped up, licking a finger mysteriously coated in brown icing.

Roared laughter circled the group until the cake was being cut and passed around.

Jake was sitting beside Brice again when he noticed Rebecca cozying up to Ian and Caleb. She was a little shy about asking Ian things, but Jake was sure she'd find a way. He scraped his plate with his fork, almost swiping the remaining icing with a finger like a three-year old.

"That was *soo* good."

"I know. Those two are evil." Brice grinned, then licked his lips. Sunlight played off the glisten, making the smooth flesh appear plump and delectably pink.

Jake bet he'd taste sweeter than the cake right then.

He blinked and leaned a scant inch away, straightening. *Wow*. He really needed to get a grip on this. He wasn't like that. He'd been married, and... And he wasn't sure who he was fooling. Confusion like this was as unknown as a penguin in Jasper.

"Um, Mr. Reynolds?"

"Hi, Becky." Those green eyes rose above Jake's head.

"Uncle Ian said you have a garden."

Oh good...gawd. Jake swallowed as what he just heard hit him square in the face.

Chapter Three

Brice tilted his head in curiosity then smiled. "I do. I was raised growing a lot of our own vegetables. As much as we could. When I moved here, it helped me feel settled faster to start my own again."

"Where are you from?"

The quiet question wasn't really an interruption, but hearing Jake ask startled Brice a little. They really hadn't spoken all that much since they'd first met. Brice focused on the man at his side. "West Virginia."

"I wondered. Every now and then I can hear your accent."

Brice laughed quietly. "Not surprising. I lived there my whole life, but learned to speak with a more moderate tone in class. If you can't sound smart to students, they're not going to even try to listen."

"And people with accents aren't smart?"

"Didn't say that." Brice winked. It was more that if the students thought they could pull one over on the teacher, they'd try, so he couldn't let them think he was one of them, even if he did know most of their families personally. "What are you trying to do?" he asked Becky, looking at her again.

"I have an agriculture paper due, a study of agribusiness and self-sustaining farming."

"Wow. For a regular grade?"

She nodded with an angsty sigh. "It's a topic I chose, but it's a large part of my final grade in one of my classes. I just didn't realize how tough it was going to be."

"The tougher, the better. Teachers respect the harder subjects. Means you put effort into your work and thought into your process. What can I do to help?"

"I need to interview you and maybe take some pictures."

Brice nodded. "Be happy to. Just let me know when and how."

"Can I email you?"

"Oh, sure. Ian and Caleb both have it, and you can come by any time you're in town with your dad."

The sigh of relief was deep. "Thank you! I'll get it from them this week. I know Terra can forward it to me."

"Sounds like a plan." He smiled as she bounced away, chirping in excitement as she explained it to Terra. They vanished into the house, probably to hit the computer.

"That's really nice of you to help her."

Brice hiked a shoulder. "It's not a problem. I'm happy to help."

"So you're a teacher and a gardener. Anything else?"

Single. But he didn't say it. He twisted on the bench to better see Jake. "Not really. The corn came from last year's garden."

"It did? It was very good."

"Thank you. I can and freeze a lot."

Jake's lips twitched. "I know the freezer department at the store."

Brice chuckled when Jake smiled innocently. "You can bring her any weekend. Just let me know. If you're coming to see Caleb, I can take her to my place for a few hours."

"Any help you can give her will be good. She wants to go to Stanford."

"Wow. She doesn't shoot low, does she?"

Jake's blue eyes warmed with pride. "We're an ambitious crowd. Our father was in judicial law, Jessie is too. Caleb is in law enforcement, and I'm a computer forensics analyst."

"Holy crap! Really?"

Those blue eyes sparkled now with mirth. "Yep. Took four years of computer analysis and engineering, plus two years of criminal justice."

"Color me impressed."

Brice noted a little hue blooming on Jake's cheeks. It looked good on the other man.

"Would you mind if I tagged along, for the gardening lesson?"

Brice met his gaze. "Of course not." Then he had an awful thought. "You do know she's safe with me, right?"

Jake's eyelashes danced, a glimmer of surprise in the blue behind them. "Why wouldn't I?"

Brice felt embarrassed now that he'd said it. He tried to backpedal. "Nothing. I think it's just a protective gene or something. I'm always around kids and their parents."

They were sitting side by side, yet Jake moved a hair closer, a sharing of confidence. "Brice, even if you weren't gay, I know I could trust her with you."

That had to be one of the nicest things anyone had ever said to him.

"How about next weekend?" he blurted. He could show Becky his garden and answer questions. *And spend time with her dad.* Yeah, totally innocent he ridiculed himself. Right that second, he honestly didn't care.

Jake relaxed, leaning on an arm on the table. "I don't see why not."

"Really? I'll make dinner for the both of you." Embarrassment was turning into a giddy elation.

"That sounds like a lot of fun. I'm sure we'll be here a lot between now and the fourth anyway. Can't let Ian down."

"Right." Brice stifled the stab of disappointment with an attempt at a jaunty smile. Of course Jake would be there for his brother-in-law. He could pretend Jake was there for Brice, though. Maybe just a little.

* * * *

When Brice said his goodbyes, Jake shook his hand and was actually sorry to see him leave. He wished Brice was staying later. The longer they'd spent talking about anything from gardening to kids, the more he'd enjoyed the conversation. There was no sign of feigned interest. He asked questions, and it wasn't to humor Jake. It was refreshing for someone to show an interest in Jake. Not in Rebecca, not in his divorce, or in his ex. Brice had seemed really impressed with his career, as much as Jake was by his gardening. They must have passed questions back and forth for over an hour as the afternoon lengthened into early evening.

Not long after Brice left, Jeannie and Wanda did as well with loving hugs and laughs. Ian, Caleb and Bethany had mostly cleaned up, the trash can full and the last plates now empty.

"Are you driving back tonight?" Caleb asked Jake. He wrapped up the trash in the kitchen to toss and filled the can with a new liner.

"Yeah, though I hate to go. It's nice having everyone together like this."

They fell silent again, lost in their own thoughts.

"Thanks for suggesting Brice to Rebecca, by the way."

"No problem. He'll help her?"

"Yeah, he wants us to come up next weekend. He'll work with her and he promised dinner."

"He's really a nice guy. He's helped Terra with a thing or two for her classes."

Jake wasn't surprised to hear that. "She's not in his?"

"Nope. Mutual agreement, and we both think she made the right move."

"Amazing how many smart kids we ended up with," Jake murmured ruefully. *Considering their gene stock.*

"Don't knock yourself, Jake. You are a great dad. Always have been. Sissy's the one who made a foolish mistake."

Jake cleared his throat. "I'm not so sure."

"What do you mean?" Caleb stopped what he was doing to stare at Jake.

"Nothing. Never mind."

"You're not still stinging over her bullshit, are you? You had nothing to do with her choices."

"No. I know." Jake straightened to his feet. "It's not her."

Caleb leaned close before Jake could escape, a caring hand on his shoulder. "If you ever need to talk to someone, you've still got us."

Jake gazed into Caleb's face. "I know. Thanks. Just nothing to discuss." At least, not that he was ready to admit.

Caleb didn't press, but Jake had a definite doubt that Caleb believed him.

Both he and Rebecca slept late Sunday morning after the drive back to Des Moines. The phone ringing made him rush getting out of the bathroom after his shower, still dripping in several places and clutching the towel.

"Hello?" he gasped, breathing heavily into the receiver after skipping through the room and not tripping over the rug.

"Hi, Jake."

"Hold on." He dropped the phone on the bed with a groan of exasperation, no longer in a hurry as he went to the bathroom and dried off. He was in no hurry at all to talk to his ex-wife.

After toweling his hair and dressing in shorts and a shirt, he gathered the phone. "What do you want, Sissy?"

"What took so long?" she snapped.

He rubbed his eyes with stiff fingers. "I was in the shower. What do you want?"

"I wanted to take Rebecca shopping next weekend. I need you to drop her off."

"We have plans next weekend."

"And I want to take her."

And here comes the bitchy pouting. Becky didn't just manufacture that pouting lip all alone. "So? Take her the weekend after. We'll be out of town next weekend."

"Again? You just took her somewhere."

"Sissy, hell's bells," he growled. "She's seventeen. What happened to spending time with her when she was ten? When she was twelve? It's not my fault you lost custody. You did that all by yourself." And almost destroyed Rebecca in the process.

"She's old enough now to have fun," she whined.

"She's also getting old enough for you to ask her if she wants to go with you. I'm not her organizer, or her secretary. She's a young woman, and you should respect that."

He heard Sissy's *hmmphed* sound of disagreement. "At least she's my daughter," she needled under her breath.

"Whatever," he retorted. It was an old ploy designed to make him angry. There was no doubt whose child she really was. Rebecca may still care for her mother, but she'd also realized she was a manipulative bitch, and had learned how to protect herself from it. "Call her later in the week and see if she wants to go with you, but this weekend is already taken."

"Fine." There wasn't so much as a goodbye shared. Just a click then silence. He hung up the phone and rubbed his face. He needed to shave, but as annoyed as he was with his ex, he'd probably slit his own throat.

"Oh, my God! Dad!"

He leaped from the bedside and hurried to his daughter's room. "What's wrong?"

He found her sitting on her bed, her laptop on her legs, her face alight with joy. "He sent me pictures!"

"Um, he who? And please don't tell me they're naked pictures." He really couldn't take much more at the moment.

"No," she groaned through a laugh. "Mr. Reynolds. He sent me about a dozen pictures and links. He's saving me so much time."

"You will still do your own research, though, right?" he pressed.

"Of course. I have to, to know what I'm actually talking about, but I wasn't expecting him to be this nice."

Jake leaned on her bedroom door frame. He frowned. He'd found Brice to be very open and good-natured. "Why not?"

Rebecca glanced up through thick, dark lashes, deep brown eyes catching his for a heartbeat. "Because he's a teacher, because he's gay, because he's an adult."

"Ah. Because you don't know him."

"Yeah, I guess so."

"That's understandable. Since he's a teacher, I think he knows when a student is being honest with what they want to achieve. As for being gay, irrelevant. And being an adult? Can't help you there, though you're pretty close to being one yourself now." He drew a slow breath. "Speaking of which..."

She glanced up when he paused.

"That was your mother on the phone. She wanted to take you out next weekend and I told her we already have plans. I also told her you're getting old enough she can ask you directly. Let me know what she's planning, but she needs to start asking you herself. I'm not the go-between."

"I've been telling her that for two years now." Rebecca grumbled impolitely. "I want to be the one she asks, not demand I attend whatever stupid errand she thinks *must* be done that day."

Jake came into the room. What he heard from his daughter was she wanted her mother's respect, and was mature enough to know when she wasn't getting it. "Why didn't you say anything? She's never been rude or mean, has she?"

"Rude is a matter of perception, but no, not mean. I guessed when you really felt it was time, you'd say something. *Annnd* because I didn't want to cause any more fights."

"Honey, you're not the reason for any fight. Your mother can be selfish, controlling and a pain, but she also cares for you."

"When she wants to," she muttered under her breath. She didn't look up from the computer screen, the emphasis clear.

Jake didn't argue, stuffing his tongue into his cheek. Unfortunately, Rebecca had nailed Sissy's dedication to motherhood in four little words.

"Getting dressed anytime soon?" He bumped the bed with a knee, addressing the fact that she was still buried beneath the sheets, changing the subject. Sometimes it was just best to leave Sissy out of their lives altogether.

"Next. I wanted to look up some ideas and found the email. Let me reply and I'll get dressed."

"Okay." He left her in her room.

Chapter Four

Brice checked his email regularly and couldn't help but smile when he got Becky's interview. She was serious about wanting to do her report right. He replied he had it and would work on it for that weekend. At least he now had something out of the ordinary to break up his week.

By the time Saturday rolled around, he was ready for the company. He'd had to send Timothy to the office again for trying to start a fight in his classroom on Tuesday. He knew the kid's home situation was rough, but he was beyond sympathizing for the young man.

He was ready for some adult conversation. Not grading papers, not worrying about grade reporting. And definitely not wanting to think about the parents who were going to blame him for their kid's lack of motivation to maybe, oh, actually do the required work and pass the class. He couldn't wave a magic wand and pass them, though he would have loved to have that magic wand to make a few disappear from his classroom.

He kept replaying the conversation he'd shared with Jake, learning about him and his family. Jake had admitted he'd been divorced for more than five years, though his ex had left him when Rebecca was not quite ten. He'd taken her to court and she'd lost in a brilliant display of parental failure. He hadn't gone into a lot of detail, and Brice hadn't pressed.

There had been a lot of pride in him for his daughter. She was ambitious and highly intelligent, but considering her father and her family, that wasn't all that surprising.

He'd just about convinced himself to put his crush and his attraction on the shelf by the time they arrived on Saturday. He knew it wasn't going to lead to anything, and he would at least get to have Jake's friendship.

That bit of wool over his eyes worked until he opened the door to him and his daughter on Saturday.

It wasn't like he'd arrived in Armani, or driving a Ferrari, or bearing gifts.

He smiled.

That was all. Jake smiled.

And Brice's heart went pitter-pat.

* * * *

"Not too early, are we?" Jake asked.

Brice blinked, his cheeks turning red. "No." He opened the door wider, muttering under his breath, but Jake couldn't catch it. "Are you sure?"

Brice looked up and straightened his shoulders. "No, you're fine. I just...lost track of time." He faced Rebecca and smiled.

Jake hoped that was true. He didn't want to impose on the man.

"Morning, Becky."

"Morning." She slid her backpack off her shoulder. "I hope this is what you meant by clothes I didn't mind getting filthy in." She waved a hand down her front, meaning the faded jeans and an old T-shirt. "I brought a change for later."

"That will work fine. I have gloves for you."

"Cool," she said.

"Would you like something to drink first? It's already getting warm out there."

Jake followed him to the kitchen, taking in the small home. It was bright, with simple lines and wide open windows. Little touches of walnut wood added character to the doorframes. The house kind of looked like Brice. Neat with simple lines. He couldn't imagine Brice needing a lot of attention-grabbing decoration. "A three-bedroom?"

"Yeah. One of the bedrooms is pretty small, but since it's just me, it doesn't matter. I use it as a library office."

Jake took the water handed to him.

"If there's not anything you need in there for outside, you can put that in the library, Becky. Left out of the kitchen and it's the second door on the right."

She sipped her water, nodding that she'd understood and trotted off to drop her pack.

"Not going to work us too hard, I hope," Jake teased, grinning mischievously at Brice.

"You'll be able to walk. Maybe." He winked and Jake laughed quietly. "Okay, ready?" he asked when Becky returned. He led them out the rear door to the half deck and down the steps to his backyard-slash-garden.

"Wow. When you said garden, I was thinking a couple of rows, a few vegetables. This is incredible," Jake said, taking it in. More than two-thirds of the yard was garden or furrowed.

"I don't have to mow," Brice said with a straight face.

"No, I can see that."

Brice opened a small shed. He reached in and reappeared with three pairs of gloves. "A must-have.

I have a few things on the agenda for today, but first, I'll show you what is where. If you have any questions, just ask."

"I brought my camera." She reached into her rear pocket and withdrew a small digital.

"Help yourself." He glanced toward Jake. "Ready to work?"

"Let's do this," he replied.

Brice's smile was broad, with a hint of evil.

Jake was surprised and impressed with Brice's resourcefulness. The garden was well set up, deeply layered and fenced in with a double layer of wire to keep out pests. He noticed as they were given the tour, that he'd dug the barrier down into the ground to stop underground thieving. Jake lost count as Brice ticked off what was there now and what he would grow through the year. There was early broccoli and spinach, potato plants that were beginning to bloom and a full row of lettuce.

"You can't eat all of this yourself," he said from where he hunkered down between rows, helping weed while Brice explained Ph balance and why he didn't use pesticides.

"I give about a quarter to the homeless shelter and they use it for their soup days."

"Really?" Jake rose up between his shoulder blades.

Brice met his gaze. "I know what it is to have nothing," he explained quietly.

Jake was positive there was a story there, but instead of prying, merely nodded.

"I also share with Ian and Jeannie. I keep my freezer stocked. One of the other benefits is taking care of this keeps me from strangling hormonal teenagers who like to think they're Muhammad Ali in my classroom."

Jake choked, leaning back on his haunches. "In the classroom?"

"Yep." He tugged up a carrot and studied it. "Just this week."

"I don't know how teachers do it these days."

"Lots of Valium," he remarked deadpan. "Lots of Valium."

Even Rebecca chuckled at that.

"These are ready to pull. Let me grab the tools and a bucket. Ever have fresh caramelized carrots for dinner?"

"Not that I can think of," Jake said.

"They're like having candy on the side." Brice stood and brushed his knees off. "After we get these up, I'll show Becky a few more things, then we can take a break. It's going to get hot back here soon."

They worked together for about another hour, pulling carrots, lettuce and a cutting a couple of the broccoli bunches.

"When we come back out, I'll show you what it takes to prepare the soil for the next seeding, because some plants need more or less."

"This is going to help me a lot," she said, wiping her brow with the back of her wrist. "I've found a few other sites that give the large bulk farming point of view, but this is really going to help."

"Good."

When Rebecca talked, Brice focused on her, really listened. Jake was sure it was just one of the facets that made him an excellent teacher as well.

With a bucket full of vegetables, Brice led them to the side of the house where an irrigation trough had been built. "I clean and strip here and then take everything inside. I don't like taking in any unwanted surprises. It does happen."

Brice showed them how to check each for insects, cleaning them with the bristle brush to remove dirt. Everything that washed away and stripped was collected beneath the trough. "What do you do with that?"

"I compost it and it becomes fertilizer. The water is siphoned back into a reservoir I built to collect rainwater to irrigate the garden. I try to not use the city supply water."

"Wow. You are so resourceful," Rebecca said with admiration.

"Definitely something you can add to your paper." She nodded at Jake's suggestion.

"Might even earn me extra points. I know the farmers don't do this. They rely on produced fertilizers and mass irrigation, usually from well-water or a main supply."

"Another way we're different, but the same, just smaller scale," Brice pointed out. "It's not really feasible for them to do this on their scale of need, but I bet they could find ways to increase or adjust to their benefit."

"Maybe," she agreed, thoughtfully.

And he just gave her a problem to consider solutions, to make her think.

"You're really good," he said quietly at his other shoulder. When Jake flicked a hinting look toward Rebecca, Brice smiled.

"I've always tried to think outside the box. This is an example. This is very sophisticated compared to the minimal gardening my grandmother started me with."

"I can see why you became a teacher."

"Oh, that," he purred with ambivalence. "That's just because I'm a glutton for punishment." He snickered then bumped shoulders with Jake. "Come on. Break time. I have ice cream and fresh peaches."

"Dad, can we keep him?"

Both Jake and Brice laughed. And he didn't miss it when Brice blushed under the compliment.

* * * *

The afternoon flew by with Brice telling them stories of his grandmother and his own childhood. By the time Brice stopped, Jake was glad for the gloves. He was sure he was going to have blisters regardless, but knew they'd have been severely worse if he hadn't worn them. Even Rebecca was winding down.

She'd snapped a ton of pictures, even a few of him and Brice, and maybe a few too many of him being silly. He made her swear those were not going into her report. He was not going to have a picture of him courting a stalk of broccoli on the Internet, or pretending to be Hamlet with a head of lettuce.

It was nice though, hearing Brice's laughter at his antics. He had a sweet laugh, not too loud, but deep, full. He also realized that this was what kept Brice in shape. All the tugging, digging, pulling and crawling, which had to be good for abdominal muscles, was a full workout.

"Did you bring a change of clothes too?" Brice asked him.

"No."

"Well, the bathroom is right here if you want to clean up. Same for Becky."

"Thanks, I appreciate it."

"You're welcome." Brice touched his arm lightly then with a smile, left him for his own bedroom to clean up.

After Rebecca changed, he went in and cleaned up as much as he could, scrubbing under his nails and all but dunking his head under the water in the sink.

While Brice put things together to start dinner, Rebecca sat at the table and talked with him about the interview.

"Need any help?" Jake offered.

"I need to sauté the onion and rice." Brice pointed to a pan and a bowl of rice.

Following his instructions, Jake thought he did well without burning anything. Soon the kitchen smelled savory and sweet and delicious. There wasn't any stress to it either. Brice was very patient with both Rebecca's gardening questions and Jake's cooking ones. It had been a long time since he'd had a home cooked meal like this, and it was comfortable. Even Rebecca was laughing and having fun. Jake realized she'd gotten over her issues of not knowing Brice Reynolds.

That evening when they left, Rebecca hugged Brice hard. "Thank you so much for all of this. Way more than I'll ever need, and it was more fun than I thought it would be."

Brice smiled for her. "You're very welcome. I'd love to know how you do on it."

"Go on out to the car. I'll be right there." Jake held the door open for her.

She slipped outside and Jake pushed until the door almost closed. "Thank you, for all you did today. Helping her, letting us both get into your garden, then dinner. My God, that was good."

34

"An appetite does wonders," he teased.

"I know it was more than that. Sissy wants to take Rebecca next weekend. Would you like to come up to my place, let me repay the favor?"

"There's nothing to repay," Brice said. "I was more than happy to help her with her paper."

Jake wasn't sure why, but wanting Brice to say yes just became the most important moment of the day. "Let me see what I can find for us to do."

Brice hesitated. "If you're sure."

Jake caught himself just before leaning forward. The want to be closer, to experience *something*, to fulfill a craving that had been slowly building within all day was simply too large to push aside any longer. Single glances, shared smiles, laughter. It had all come to this.

He swallowed and simply nodded. "I'm sure."

When he thought he'd forget all the things he felt last weekend, when he was positive it was wrong and he was just noticing things about the other man because he was actually getting to know him, Jake realized something about himself that he hadn't considered in two decades.

He was attracted to men.

He was *attracted* to Brice. And right that moment, before he left, he really wanted to kiss him goodbye. It was a bit startling, and such a rush, it made him uncomfortable.

Instead, he took a short step away to open the door again. "Call me later in the week when you know for sure and I'll give you directions."

When Brice agreed, he managed to walk out the door for the car, turning once to wave as he slid behind the wheel.

The entire drive home with Rebecca silent in the passenger seat reading over what she'd written with Brice's help, his only thought was he regretted not taking that kiss.

Chapter Five

"Caleb?"

"Hmm?"

Jake swallowed. Now that he had his brother on the phone clutched in his hand, he wasn't sure how to go about bringing up the reason he'd convinced himself to call in the first place. Two days ago, he'd spent hours with Brice, laughing, having fun, admiring the shine of sunlight in his pale hair, the sparkle of green in his eyes, and grateful for the patience he'd shown his daughter. Both the gardener and the teacher in him had been a wealth of information, sharing his knowledge and even showing her the differences in the details, taking time and making the effort when he didn't have to do a fraction of what he'd done.

And for two nights now, Jake had been dreaming of him. It was driving him crazy. This hadn't happened in nearly twenty years.

"Still want to listen?" His voice was a mere whisper of what it usually was. He was locked in his bedroom, Rebecca watching TV or something. He sat on the edge of his bed, fisting the blankets between restless fingers since there was no cord for the phone.

"Okay. Ian isn't home yet." There was a weight of seriousness in his brother's voice proving Jake had all of his attention. "What do you want to talk about?"

Jake cleared his throat and stared at the far wall. "Would you have a problem with a... Well, with me, if..."

Caleb's humored chuckle rumbled through the phone. "Jake, I'd never have a problem with anything about you."

"Even if I was bi?" He closed his eyes, waiting for any reaction, expecting the worst.

"I'm gay. You really think I care?"

His shoulders sagged with relief. Not a total disregard, but a less than troubled response. That was good. He'd hoped Caleb would be the most understanding in their family.

"It's not the same," Jake said. And that was the little fact that was causing him terror. This *wasn't* the same thing.

"You're right. It's not the same, but it makes no difference to me if you find either women or men attractive. You've known since I was thirteen that I have no interest in women. They're aesthetically beautiful, like a waterfall, or a star-filled sky but to embrace? To become intimate? No, thank you."

A tightness in Jake's chest relaxed. "So you don't think I'm too old to find men suddenly attractive?"

"Jake?"

"Yes?"

"Is it really suddenly?"

Jake didn't blink. It took a few seconds to find the air in his lungs to answer. "No," he finally croaked. The quiet voice inside was agreeing. It had always been there, just never acted on after Sissy got pregnant. He'd made his choice. The reasoning behind that choice was tearing him apart now. He hadn't been wrong, but he hadn't been right either. All he knew was Rebecca would never be a mistake.

After a moment of silence, Jake heard, "Tell me something. If Rebecca hadn't happened, would you have married Sissy?"

"I've asked myself that too," Jake whispered.

"So, answer yourself. I think you're due a little truth. And when you have your answer, go for what you want. I was so damned lucky to find Ian after John. If you find someone who makes you happy, then..."

"What?"

"Well, Jake. The rest is up to you."

He hung up a few minutes later, trembling slightly, and scared shitless.

* * * *

Brice barely looked up from his planner as students filed into his room, rowdy as the last hour of the school day approached. Fridays were like that. Everyone was ready to beat feet and hit the weekend running. He wasn't any different. He was going to call Jake when he got home and make sure Saturday was still open. He'd been thinking about it all week and finally decided he wanted the man's friendship if nothing else. Friends weren't falling out of the sky and the fact that Jake was from Caleb's stock told Brice plenty.

He'd really enjoyed the previous Saturday spent in the garden with both him and his daughter. Rebecca had asked a slew of intelligent questions, and a few silly ones. She had a warm sense of humor. Brice didn't think he was off the mark believing she would have received that from her father. They'd had an enjoyable day and had shared a great afternoon and meal when they were done working in the garden. He'd learned more about Jake's branch of work, and Rebecca had shared her dreams of attending Stanford, researching different tangents of law for herself. She was looking toward the humanitarian angles. Jake had high hopes for her, and honestly Brice could see it in her to do well.

Yes, he was deeply attracted to Jake, but he also recognized the futility of it. The man had been married. There had also been no hint of attraction in Jake for Brice. He'd been kind, fun, and charming. More of the Drew family's genes than being personally intended for Brice.

The bell sounded and he didn't notice any empty seats with a sweeping glance. "Zane, close the door, please." The last student in the front row stood and shut the door. "Thank you."

Brice stood from his desk, and faced the chalkboard, writing as his thoughts churned, trying to hang in there long enough to get to three o'clock. "Continuing from the chapter from yesterday, let's see who read the homework. Who can give me examples of the pivotal environments—" He paused to look over his shoulder when the room door opened. "You're late, Timothy. Please sit down. I'll see you after class."

"Yes, Mr. Reynolds." The thick built redhead took a step to do as he was told and Brice raised his arm to write more, dismissing Timothy. They'd already locked horns twice, and the last time had been for Timothy trying to start a fight in class with another student. He'd sent them both to the office. He did not want that kind of disruption in his classroom.

A sharp scream raised the hair on his arms. Brice spun, his vision blocked by a body as he tried to figure out why someone was screaming in his classroom.

Air gushed from his chest as he was body tackled into the chalkboard with a rattling thud.

"Fucking faggot," Timothy snarled. He pinned Brice with a full shoulder and had managed to shove an arm upward against Brice's throat in the matter of a heartbeat.

A silvery flash of something metallic caught the light fanning through the windows before it went out of sight. Brice fought, kicking upward with a knee. His left arm had become pinned, shoved between his chest and Timothy's. He was at a horrible disadvantage in that position to protect himself. His blind kick glanced a blow and then Brice felt the jabbed prick of sharpness right below his ribs. Pain blinded him in a shocked exhale of excruciating, blistering agony.

Realization and motion were instantaneous. Timothy was going to kill him, stab him right there in the classroom. He gasped and shoved but Timothy outweighed him. Then the youth was ripped away, literally swept off his feet at the knees. Brice sagged to the floor, drawing air. Another one of the girls screamed. God, he wished they wouldn't do that.

"Call nine-one-one," he managed, holding a hand to his left front, grimacing as sharp pain burst with each breath. Slick blood welled into his hand. *That is not good.*

Timothy was wrestling to move and it looked like half the class had dog-piled him to keep him right where he was.

"Mr. Reynolds!" One of the women teachers scurried into the room, falling at his side to help. "Class, please, give him some room. Angela, wet some paper towels. Find the principal." She noticed the writhing mass of limbs. "Is that the one who did this?"

Several nodded.

"I will fail the first person to let him off the floor."
It was said in absolute chilling finality. A couple more
sat on the pile for emphasis. Grunts and shouts were
muffled and wholly ignored. "Hold on, Brice. Let me
look." He was eased to his back, something lumpy,
probably a backpack, slid into place to rest his head
on. The ceiling wavered then rolled, and he closed
his eyes. "You need stitches at least. It doesn't look
deep. Just relax." Mrs. Vickers' tone was calm. It
couldn't be all that bad, then. He felt steady pressure
on his side and chest where the pain was. He was just
trying to breathe. It really hurt to breathe deeply.

It didn't take long for more people to show up,
the police, other students. Eventually the crowded
room was cleared and Timothy was taken away. Brice
followed on a gurney.

He began to get the idea that maybe things
weren't as stable as he'd first thought, that he needed
more than a few stitches in the ambulance when they
applied the oxygen mask. Then they gave him a shot
in the IV and he really didn't know anything else.

* * * *

"Dad! Uncle Caleb is on the phone."

"Okay." He walked into the living room from the
kitchen where he'd been choosing what to make for
dinner and took the phone when she handed it to
him. "Hello?"

"Hey, Jake. I don't know if anyone called you or
not, but Brice is in the hospital."

Jake sank slowly down to the couch. His skin
went cold. "What happened?"

"One of his seniors attacked him with a knife.
He's out of surgery. It wasn't bad, but it was deep

enough to nick something. We're letting close friends know."

"His family?" Jake queried.

"In an answer, no."

Jake had guessed but hadn't heard it directly from Brice. "That explains a lot." He bit at his lip. "He was going to come here this weekend." Except he hadn't called, and Jake hadn't been sure he was really going to take him up on the offer. He'd seemed to want to, but there'd been silence all week. Jake had tried to not get his hopes up. He still wasn't exactly sure just *what* he was hoping for either. He wasn't any closer to unwinding his own troubles even after talking to his brother about all the new questions plaguing him.

"He'll be home tomorrow morning," Caleb offered.

"Is anyone there with him now?" He glanced upward when he noticed Rebecca standing at the hallway entrance, watching him questioningly.

"I don't know. Ian and I are going to see him for a few minutes tonight to make sure he has a way home."

Jake nodded. "Okay. Should I call him? No... Never mind."

Caleb sighed his name.

"No. It's okay."

"If you say so," Caleb replied, less than convinced. "Want me to call you later?"

"Yes, please," fell out in a rush. They said their goodbyes then hung up.

"What's wrong?" Rebecca asked, eyeing him with concern.

"Brice was injured by a student this afternoon."

"No!" She snapped straight from her usual teenager slouch. "What did they do to him?" Anger flamed in her eyes.

Brice's avenging angel. Her reaction warmed him, that she actually cared about him as a friend. "Apparently one of the students pulled a knife on him in class. He's okay."

"But... Is he in the hospital?"

"Yes." He stood, anxious and unable to pinpoint all the reasons behind it. "Caleb will call later and let me know how he's doing." He smiled for his daughter. He tried to anyway. "Let's get dinner started."

"Okay," she replied, stilted motions proving she was obviously torn over what she should do. He felt exactly the same way.

They managed to get through dinner, though it was withdrawn and tense with worry. He swore he looked at the time every five minutes, almost tapping his fingers waiting for Caleb's call.

They both jumped when it finally came. "Hello?" Rebecca hovered nearby as he stood by the couch this time.

"Okay. He's to be released in the morning about nine. The doctor said there hadn't been a lot of damage, but the knife sliced him at a sharp angle. It managed to pierce his diaphragm and nick his lower lung, so they had to make sure all his innards were okay."

"Will someone be staying with him?"

"I haven't heard if it's necessary, but he probably should take a few days to recover. He's going to be at home for at least that long before going back to class."

Jake wasn't all that surprised. With an injury like that, he likely wouldn't be moving much.

"You know what, though. I bet he could use a friend to keep him company. In case he can't lift or anything like that. A day or two," Caleb mused.

Jake nodded, knowing he was being pulled by the nose and not even mad about it.

"Ian and I can stop by, but I'm on shift and with Brock and Jackson working for him, he's keeping the shop open later on Saturdays now."

"I don't want to get in the way, Caleb. What if he doesn't want me, or anyone, there?"

"Be at our house by eight. We'll all go, so he knows we give a shit."

Jake heard the smile in his brother's voice.

"I'll be there."

"Thought you would be," Caleb drawled. "See you in the morning. Bye."

"Bye."

He disconnected the call.

"Well?"

He tilted his chin to face his daughter, his mind ticking off a list for himself to stay overnight. "Call your mother and let her know she'll have to come get you here. I have to be in Jasper in the morning. Oh, and take a change of clothes. I'll be back on Sunday."

"You will call and tell me how he is, won't you?" She sat on the couch and he did as well, giving her his full attention. She plucked at her shorts, looking at him through her lashes, and looking far from seventeen. More like his little girl. "I liked him Dad. He didn't laugh at me, or make me feel stupid, and he had some great stories."

He opened his mouth, ready to agree with her and then some. He'd really liked Brice too, maybe in ways he was finally realizing he wanted to explore. He put a hand on her thigh, stifling all the roiling thoughts before he said something he couldn't take back, before he said something he didn't fully understand himself. "Yes, I'll call." When she pinned him with a stare, he added, "Promise."

Chapter Six

Jake followed behind Ian and Caleb through the automatic hospital doors. He'd arrived at their house a little after eight and then rode with them to pick up Brice. Caleb swore it would be okay and that he wouldn't think they were ganging up on him.

It seemed fairly quiet for a Saturday morning, a few nurses in the hallways and two at the station as they passed it.

When they reached Brice's room on the second floor, he was sitting up in a wheelchair already. "Hey, pincushion. They letting you out yet?" Caleb joked, walking in and offering a hand.

Brice shook hands, smiling broadly for all of them. Jake wasn't sure but he swore Brice's green eyes might have lit from within when their gazes connected. He knew he didn't want to let Brice's hand go. He stood at Brice's side instead in support.

"Ten minutes. The nurse is getting copies of my release and follow-up signed."

Caleb occupied the time by asking about the stuffed animals piled on his lap. Brice blushed hotly, and Jake thought it was the cutest thing to see.

"Several of the students and even a couple of the teachers came to see me last night." The frivolity in his tone dried up as he explained, "Timothy is being charged as an adult for assault with a deadly weapon. Would you believe his brother did the exact same thing about five years ago to a sophomore? Pulled a knife on him and tried to kill him."

Jake saw Caleb and Ian share a startled stare.

"The same family?" Ian asked. "Un-fucking-believable."

"Their father is hyper-homophobic and when I sent Timothy to the office for almost starting a fight in my class, his dad actually put the blame on me."

Caleb frowned. "Timothy's father has also been brought in for questioning. There were several charges being considered when I saw the report. Timothy said his father was the one who gave him the knife yesterday morning before school. Had the balls to tell him not to come home without it covered in homo blood."

"Holy shit," Jake breathed. "And here I thought Jasper was actually pretty tame." What if that brat kid had succeeded? His heart tripped and a fist formed by his hip as he realized just how close Brice had been to death.

Caleb smirked. "Usually we are, but we do have a few loud and vengeful sour apples."

"At least Paul moved. He couldn't handle living next to our den of inequity and vile sin." Ian rolled his eyes.

"No loss," Caleb added. "Since he's left, the council has actually calmed a lot. He always stirred them for nonsense issues."

Another body almost barreled into the room, stopping short with the squeak of sneakers and a small-voiced yelp. "Oh, hello there. Seems the party arrived while I was gone." The nurse winked at Brice. "And a handsome-loaded party at that."

"Hi, Tina," Caleb said, laughing as he shook her hand. "Being good?"

"Hells no. What's the fun in that?" She opened the file gripped in her fingers. "All right, Mr. Reynolds, you are officially out of here." She handed him pages as she ticked them off. Soon all the paper she'd held was on Brice's lap. "Okay, let me get him popping wheelies down the corridor." Jake stepped away, giving the nurse room to get to the push bars of the wheelchair. "I feel like a mama duck. Line up!"

"I like her," Jake murmured to Caleb.

He chuckled in Nurse Tina's direction. "She's been here forever and I don't think I've ever seen her not like this."

The group trooped obediently down the hall to the first floor breezeway. "Let me get the car," Caleb offered, jogging ahead.

"Thank you, Tina. You and your team were really nice, though you'll have to forgive me if I don't rush to come stay at your place again." Brice smiled upward.

Tina chortled quietly, patting his shoulder affectionately. "No offense taken. Just get your rest and do what the instructions tell you to do."

"Don't worry. We're here to make sure he doesn't lift a finger," Jake said.

Brice looked up questioningly, but Jake motioned with a hand to redirect his attention because Caleb was rolling the car to a stop in front of them. It took a few minutes to get Brice settled and his belongings in the trunk, then with all four in the car, they left the hospital.

* * * *

"Thank you, all of you, for coming to bust me out," Brice teased. He hadn't expected to see Jake, but he wasn't going to complain. It was actually kind of sweet that he was there.

"Well, I'm on shift later, and Ian is going back to the garage, so actually Jake will be with you for a couple of days."

"If that's okay with you," Jake quickly interjected. The show of worry in his expression warmed Brice. Like it mattered. Like *he* mattered.

"Completely," Brice said, giving the man at his side a soft smile. He let his head rest on the back of the seat, kind of loose as he talked quietly. "I was going to call yesterday. I was looking forward to seeing you."

"Another weekend," Jake said, and it sounded like a promise to Brice.

"Jake, I'm going to drop you off to get your car. Ian has to get back to the shop. Do you have anything you need picked up, Brice?" Caleb spoke from the front seat, tugging his distracted focus that way.

"I think the hospital called in some prescriptions at the pharmacy," he replied.

"Anything you want for the house? Use me while you got me." Jake winked and Brice nearly melted.

If you only knew how I'd use you. He swallowed and shook his head. His thoughts were scrambled gazing at the man beside him on the seat. Being medicated wasn't helping him keep his internal digressions from becoming an external demonstration either.

"Okay," Jake said when they pulled up outside Caleb's. "I'll be over as soon as I'm done."

They both waved as they pulled away, Ian on his motorcycle and Jake by his car. Brice cracked a huge yawn as he and Caleb pulled up in front of his home a few minutes later.

"I saw that," Caleb joked, flashing a smile in the rearview mirror to Brice.

Brice grinned and shrugged. He knew it would take a few days to get back to some semblance of a normal speed. He used the open car door to get to his feet, ensuring he was steady enough to stand before trying to let go.

"Need help?" Caleb asked walking around to his side.

"Let me just lean on you. I think I can handle that. Didn't realize this would make walking hard."

"It's just because you're tender in places that shouldn't be."

He offered an elbow and Brice didn't balk at all about using it for support. "All my stuff?"

"Let's get you inside first," Caleb offered.

It only took a few minutes to get Brice and all his get-well gifts inside. "Do you want me to stay until Jake gets back?"

Brice waved a hand from the couch where he stretched out. "Go ahead. Just leave the door unlocked. He shouldn't be too long. Oh, and could you set the phone here?" He motioned to the end table.

Caleb went to the kitchen and grabbed the phone, leaving it by Brice's head. "Anything else?"

Brice nestled down into the cushions. "No. I think I'm going to rest. I'll listen for Jake."

"Okay. We'll see how you're doing later." Caleb turned for the door.

"Caleb?"

"Yeah?" His hand rested on the knob.

"Thanks for everything you guys have done, not just today."

He smiled kindly and then walked out the door keeping Brice from embarrassing himself in his current state of dopiness.

Brice let his eyes flutter shut, welcoming the calm quiet of his recuperation to push aside the aches in his chest and side. He wasn't sure how long he faded in and out, but he slowly blinked his eyes open to find Jake drawing a blanket over him.

"Hi there. Feeling okay?" Jake asked gently.

"Groggy." Brice smacked his lips. "Thirsty."

"Stay put. I have your prescriptions. Do you need the pain one yet?"

Brice took a slow breath. "Not yet."

"Okay. Rest. I'll be right back."

Jake helped him sit when he returned to take his required pill and drink what he wanted, then let him get comfortable again. He slid off Brice's glasses and placed them on the table out of the way. "Do you mind if I call Rebecca and let her know you're okay? She was really upset when she heard about what had happened last night."

"Go right ahead. Give her the number. You don't have cell phones?"

"Never needed one really. I don't believe we need to be available twenty-four seven."

"Damn, I like you," Brice murmured, giggling quietly. He thought only the pain medications were supposed to make him loopy. Maybe it hadn't faded yet. Maybe he was still at its mercy, or maybe he was just lax enough to actually say what he was thinking. That was totally probable. He was also pretty sure he was loosely grinning.

"I like you too," Jake replied while a warm touch breezed over Brice's forehead. "Rest. I'll figure out dinner when I see what you can eat."

Brice lifted a limp hand to wave in a general direction. "Caleb put it...all over...there somewhere."

"Rest...cute stuff."

Brice was positive he'd made it up, but he still loved the way it sounded in Jake's voice. *Cute stuff.* He dozed off smiling and dreaming of Jake.

At one point, he sniffed and smelled delicious aromas, cooking and spices. He moaned trying to wake up. It smelled really good, and his stomach was telling him he should eat something.

"Brice? Can you wake up?"

He drew a deep breath, wincing when the action pulled on things it shouldn't have. "I'm trying," he mumbled.

"Those drugs they gave you are serious. Good thing you're home for a while."

"Anti-inflammatory gobbledy-gook," he managed, rolling his head on the pillow. Huh. When did a pillow show up on the couch?

Jake laughed, interrupting his thoughts. "Well, I doubt it's anywhere near as good as yours, but I put together a soup for you. The doctor's instructions said to keep food light for the first twenty-four to forty-eight hours."

Brice finally blinked his eyes opened, and as he stared upward, Jake carefully slid his glasses into place on his nose.

"There. Can you see me now?" he intoned in that phone commercial voice. Jake's smiling face was an amazing thing to focus on when he woke up. "Let's get you up so you can eat."

"I didn't feel like this leaving the hospital," he grumbled.

"You're home now and really able to heal. Makes a world of difference."

Brice wasn't sure this was an improvement. He felt weaker, and more than a little dazed. This wasn't exactly what he'd imagined *healing* would feel like.

Together they straightened Brice on the couch with smooth pulls and adjustments. Jake tucked the blanket he'd been sleeping under beneath his legs then propped a tray on Brice's lap. "Do I know where this came from?"

"I bought it today. Thought it was cute, and it would be useful."

It was a handled wooden lap tray with fat bees painted over large colorful flowers.

"It made me think of your garden," Jake said quietly.

Brice caught the red on his cheekbones. There was a slight tan, or maybe an olive tone to Jake's skin and when he blushed, it was sexy as hell.

"I love it," Brice told him.

"Okay, then try the soup while you're still feeling magnanimous."

Brice smirked. He blew on a large spoonful of broth and chopped vegetables. And sighed in bliss as the warmth bathed his throat and his chest. "Amazing. Really good."

The pleasure those two words brought up in Jake's features made Brice's breath catch and it was absolutely unrelated to the soreness of his body.

Chapter Seven

Brice awoke startled to be in his bed. He hardly remembered getting there. As the sleep cobwebs dissipated, he began to piece it together. He'd slept most of Saturday on the couch, Jake nearby either reading or watching the television turned down low. He'd eaten more of the soup then Jake had helped him get to bed. He had been walking better, just slowly.

He touched the stitches below his ribs with light fingers. It was a little hard to believe, how close to death he'd come in a matter of seconds. A single person able to cause so much harm, who *wanted* to cause harm.

He was eternally grateful to all those in the classroom who'd helped him, and the student who'd managed to knock Timothy off his feet. It turned out sending him to the principal had set him up for disciplinary action, which had put him on the short list for losing his college scholarship. It was a donated scholarship, and one of the rules was a clean record.

Now he'd gone beyond losing his scholarship. He'd been expelled, arrested and charged, which would permanently be on his record as an adult. All because Timothy's father was an intolerant fuck. The nut didn't fall far from the tree in their family at all. All of them had problems from what Brice had gleaned from the others.

Brice closed his eyes and exhaled. He hadn't broadcast his preferences, but he hadn't tried to be something he wasn't, either. There wasn't even anyone in his life to make the presumption that he *was* gay.

A muted knock on the front door floated through the house, followed by the sound of it opening and voices. A moment or two later it closed. Soft tapping sounded at his bedroom door next.

"I'm awake," he called. He inched up on the bed as Jake opened the door to peek in.

"Morning," he said, all smiles. "How'd you sleep?"

"Good. You were okay?" He felt bad that Jake was relegated to the couch. He didn't have a second bed anywhere, hidden or otherwise.

"Yeah." Jake widened the door to stand in the frame.

He was wearing baggy cargo shorts and a sassy black pullover open at the throat. Casual and scrumptious. "Who was at the door?"

"Jeannie. She and Wanda sent you something. I put it in the kitchen."

"Thanks." He swung his blankets out of the way and twisted to place his feet on the floor.

"Need help?"

Brice shook his head. "I feel stronger. Just tender."

"No doubt. Okay. Let me know if you need a hand."

"Hey, uh, Jake?"

He paused in leaving, twisting to meet Brice's gaze, a question hanging between them.

"Thanks. It was really nice of you to come stay with me."

"Not a problem." He left and Brice managed to shuffle himself into the bathroom to make himself presentable. Getting dressed was still too much work. At least his pajamas were in good shape, no holes in the crotch or rips in the knee. He'd tried to avoid letting things get to that condition since being on his own and able to make his own budgets and decisions.

By the time he reached the kitchen, there was an ache in his chest from the exertions. "How long before I feel human?" he muttered. He propped himself against a chair with a firm hand.

"At least a week, but about four to fully heal."

He groaned. "I can't miss a week of class. God only knows what a sub will let them get away with."

A full glass of apple juice appeared. "Drink. We'll worry about work in another day or two."

"Yes, mother." Brice sat at the table and was treated to a plate of scrambled eggs and sliced tomatoes.

"This is really good. It's been a while since anyone has cooked for me." He took another mouthful, savoring. Jake had done something to the eggs, herbs or something, and shredded cheese. Either way, they were delicious. He licked at his lip, trying to catch a thread of melted goodness.

"Thank you." Jake slid out a chair and joined him. "Rebecca is glad you're home and said to tell you hi."

"You have a wonderful daughter." Brice watched Jake thoughtfully. "You haven't mentioned her mother. Is she still around?"

"She is. Rebecca is with her this weekend."

"I take it your split wasn't a good one?" he asked.

Jake slowed his eating. Though he didn't really show any other expression on his face, the restrained anger was clear in Jake's voice.

"No, it wasn't. She is and always has been a very spoiled person. She went to college specifically to find a husband. She got me when she became pregnant with Rebecca."

Brice gaped, but held his tongue when Jake shook his head.

"No, not tricked. We always used protection, but it failed, and six months later, we were married. We lasted until I came home from a weekend at the lake with my brothers to find her stuff moved out. Rebecca was nine." He paused, gathering his thoughts, or deciding how much to say. "We separated and started going through the process of the divorce. Then I got a call one afternoon asking for an earlier pickup on her weekend, only it wasn't from Sissy. It turned out she was paying a babysitter to keep Rebecca from Friday afternoon until Sunday, which was when Sissy would then pick her up and supposedly return her to me as though they'd been together the whole weekend. She was stone cold busted. It wasn't the first time she'd done that either. I filed after that and won full custody on abandonment charges. Motherhood wasn't what she'd planned on, just the husband part. The ugly was just beginning."

Brice reached and covered Jake's hand resting on the table. "I'm sorry. You didn't do anything wrong, Jake. You raised an incredible daughter full of compassion and intelligence. I believe she's a lot like her father, more than her mother," he added sincerely.

Jake's shoulders sagged with a deep exhale.

Brice wiped his mouth quickly with a napkin then stood. With a tender hand, he grasped Jake by the arm and tugged until he gave in and stood with him.

"You are not to blame," Brice enunciated, gazing into blue eyes. "You're an incredible man, a special person. Never forget that." Carefully, because he wasn't sure of his own limits or what Jake's reaction would be, he wrapped arms around Jake and hugged him.

Slowly, Jake copied him and clung.

"Not too tight," he rasped, burying his face into the crook of Jake's shoulder. The scent of skin was intoxicating.

When Jake went to release him, Brice shook his head. "No. Just don't squeeze the stuffing out of me." He grinned, including the laughter he felt to his voice.

"I think I can promise not to do that," Jake replied. The press of his smile on skin warmed Brice through.

Then Brice relaxed, chest to chest, body heat to body heat. Jake did the same and suddenly he was in heaven. "Hugs are therapeutic," he pointed out. And Jake's hug felt divine.

"Not too tight?" Jake asked. The brush of his breath burned the skin beneath Brice's ear. "Don't want to hurt you."

Brice swallowed. "I'm fine. You?"

"Fine." Yet after a minute if not longer neither moved, simply standing in the embrace of arms.

Slowly, almost hesitantly nervous, the hand stretched across Brice's back splayed out, as though seeking. Brice sighed, soaking up the contact. That hand swept up, then down, caressing skin that shivered with the tentative pass. When Brice would have expected Jake to become uncomfortable with the continued intimacy, he swore he felt the softest tingle of lips at the edge of his jaw. Another breath between them, then Jake began to untangle himself from around Brice.

He was sorry to let him go. It had been years since he'd been held so close by someone he cared about.

"Thank you," Jake said tenderly. He drifted a hand up Brice's arm to cup his neck. Blue eyes tangled with green in a heart-stopping moment.

Brice almost held his breath waiting for the kiss that hung expectantly in the air between them.

* * * *

Jake held Brice in his palm, swallowing slowly when he couldn't move, when he could hardly blink. An ache he had never anticipated and couldn't begin to break down to understand gripped his gut and twisted. A resurgence of the heat he'd felt a week ago staring into those eyes. Raw and needy. Jake was careful in how he examined it.

He moved his thumb, a light stroke, tearing his gaze away from the green of Brice's eyes to follow it, to study the motion and the signals he was getting. Right where he'd so innocently pressed with his lips in discovery. Soft skin, and the slight abrasion of facial hair, but even it felt soft. His jaw was strong, but not too angular. *Pretty.* That was the word, but he never would have thought to use it to describe a guy. But with those bold eyes and just the faintest hint of freckles on his nose, and an almost angelic face, pretty was the only thing that came to mind.

"Amazing," Jake whispered, ripping away from the magic of skin touching skin to stare into watchful eyes.

Brice's lips parted slightly, every nuance electric as nerves sizzled into awakened awareness. Jake couldn't say he'd been celibate since his divorce, because he hadn't been. However, the notion that he'd feel this much heat, this much desire with a guy hadn't crossed his mind as a possibility. He certainly hadn't felt it since...

He blinked and almost like a snap of fingers, sorrow and dejection weighed down Brice's gaze. Where anticipation and need had made them glow, now they were reflective behind the flat pane of his glasses.

Brice rolled a shoulder. "Glad to help. I meant it though. Never doubt for a minute what you have in your daughter."

Jake watched as Brice palmed his plate and took it to the sink to rinse. Brice touched his arm, a fleeting contact only conveying kindness, to then walk gingerly into the living room. Sitting carefully, he claimed his spot on the couch, watching TV by himself.

Jake cleaned up, aware that too much would exhaust Brice while he was still recovering, then, when he was finished he wasn't sure what else to do. He wasn't sure what to do about the signals, either. About the surge of blood or...want. He knew he was attracted to Brice. He had accepted that much, since he hadn't been able to forget him since the barbecue at Caleb's. Jake really had no answers on how to deal with it. Or if he dared to hope Brice felt anything in return.

Or what Jake would do if he did. He felt frozen and unsure. Keeping busy in the kitchen was just a cover to hide his more turbulent thoughts.

The phone rang and Brice reached to the table to pick it up. "Hello? Hi Rebecca. Yes, I'm doing much better. Thank you. Yes, he is. One sec."

Brice waved the phone toward Jake. He cleared the living room and clasped it. "Hi there. How's it going at your mom's?"

"Horrid," she whispered. "I'm hiding in the bathroom."

"What's wrong?" Jake asked, sitting on the couch next to Brice.

"She's being a bitch, Dad. We went shopping, and you know our tastes aren't exactly the same." He knew that for a fact, actually. That was code for Sissy didn't approve of Rebecca's choices and probably scorned everything. And then refused to buy her a thing. Even though her care was split, Sissy made *everything* an ordeal. "Then she threw a fit because I needed to stay overnight, even though I told her it was an emergency. Apparently it screwed up some major plan she had with her boyfriend. He didn't seem put out by it, just her. Next time, let me stay at home. Please?"

"Well, honey, you're almost eighteen. If that's what you want, then you're perfectly able to make that decision." She was old enough now, but she'd been going to Sissy's to begin with. He rubbed his forehead with stiff fingers. Honestly, would one night have killed his ex-wife? Just like she loved to throw in his face, Rebecca was *her* child too. He even had the DNA testing done when she was born to prove it. He'd never told Sissy, but really, he wasn't going to marry her blindly. "What is she doing?"

"The usual stuff about you, and when I tell her she's wrong, she goes into a tantrum. She really lost it when I told her about last weekend and Brice."

Jake could only imagine. Since Rebecca didn't turn into a mini-clone of Sissy, a spoiled drama queen, she'd always resented it and blamed Jake's so-called leniency in how he'd raised her. Which meant Rebecca didn't hold the same intolerant resentments and issues. Really, Jake hadn't even known that about her until Caleb started dating John, since they lived too far away to see often. By then it was too late, by a long shot. Sissy had barely tolerated Caleb after that. It hadn't made her exactly well-liked or wanted within the family circle, either.

"Okay, look. You know where I keep the cash in my bureau. Get a cab and go home. I'll be home this evening at the latest."

"Thank you, Dad. I'll behave."

"I know you will. Just lock the door."

"Love you," she breathed.

"You too. Be careful getting home."

She managed a quick goodbye then the phone went quiet.

"Sounds like staying over didn't go over," Brice intoned sympathetically.

"No. I should have known she'd use the change of plans to cause problems."

"I'm sorry." Brice lowered his gaze, all but slouching on the couch cushion.

Jake curled a palm over Brice's closest shoulder. "Hey, don't apologize. I'm happy to be here. She would use a stubbed toe to throw a hissy-fit if it got her something. I wish I'd known it before I married her, hell, before I had sex with her, but I was young and I wasn't being too picky."

Brice smirked, the corner of his mouth twitching. "I've heard that happens."

"I guess you weren't quite as wild with your family." Jake began to rub the shoulder under his hand.

"No. I wasn't out to them until I was actually out of the house for quite some time. I had three friends who knew and were sworn to secrecy. I think a few others guessed. I didn't play sports, I wasn't exactly into dating. I went stag to the prom."

Jake inched closer, curling the hand on Brice's shoulders around him to draw him into his chest. Brice was hesitant, but he eventually found a comfortable position. "Let's see what's on. You're next pill isn't due for a while."

"Yay," he quipped. But he settled into place, curled up against Jake's chest. The surprising thing—or maybe not so surprising at all—was how much Jake liked him being there.

Chapter Eight

Brice lifted his head, blinking blearily. Then he realized why his vision wasn't improving. His glasses were gone. He hunted near his head with a careful, seeking hand only to draw to a stop as he realized his pillow was in fact a chest. A slow rise and fall confirmed it.

He was asleep *on top of* Jake. He shivered as more sensations woke up nerves. He remembered cuddling, then Jake straddling him to let Brice stretch out, then... He must have dozed off and Jake had held him, protectively cocooned between two arms as they both slept on the couch. He was definitely lying on top of the man, their legs entwined with one of Brice's arms tucked against the couch and Jake's frame.

His thoughts leaped into instant turmoil. Stay like that? Try to extricate himself? The strong arms surrounding him were sublime, comforting. Clothing warmed by skin. Cotton, and the fainter scent of deodorant. He couldn't decide with longing and desire flooding his bloodstream.

Brice inched forward, drawn close enough to nose into Jake's throat. He mumbled a staggered breath then a sigh in his sleep. Brice wasn't going to do anything. Just wanted to be closer. He rested his head on Jake's shoulder, and only realized how that adjustment affected his position when a certain body part on Jake began to show interest.

Those same arms cinched a hair, as though loath to let him slip away. Brice didn't want to move at all. He shifted to keep pressure off the left side of his body, mainly resting on his right ribcage. So long as he didn't move too quickly or add too much strain, he wasn't uncomfortable.

As though sharing the sentiment, one of Jake's bare feet crooked over Brice's calf. Relaxing, he propped himself on a taut shoulder to keep off his ribcage, but the angle brought him to within a breath of the same neck he'd just wanted to get closer to. Shaved smooth. He tilted and closed his eyes as his lips connected to that skin. As lightly as Jake had earlier. His heart tripped and a short gasp slipped free as awareness zinged to his core.

Jake hummed a sweet purr. Which, right or wrong, only compelled Brice to do it again. Lingering. Enjoying. Breathing him in. Arms tightened and hands splayed wide on Brice's back. Drifting in taste, scent, and sensation, Brice teased at flesh with the tip of his tongue, shivering when the hard tattoo of a heartbeat danced for him. Slow exploration turned into butterfly kisses. Tender hands grew bolder, caressing.

Brice raised his head at an angle and suddenly Jake's lips were there. He jerked slightly, opening his eyes to find Jake's. Not needlepoint sharp, but there was definite want and desire swirling in the blue. Jake cupped Brice's cheek, a thumb stroking him. The gaze before him was adoring, soft, wanting.

Jake urged him close and together they erased the small gap keeping them apart. Brice's eyes closed, falling shut as the rest of him felt weightless. The kiss was sweet and tender. Jake's palm was gentle, that thumb of his leaving sparks in his wake, like he couldn't get enough of the simple touch. Like he was learning.

It didn't last long, a few heartbeats until the pillowed caress of lips was broken. Brice blinked open his eyes and almost flinched at the wide-eyed stare pinned on him.

"Is that—"

"I'm sorry!"

They spoke at the same time. Jake's brow drew tight in confusion. "Why are you sorry?"

Unfortunately, Brice couldn't just leap away, or slink under the couch. He was mortified. The heat flooding his face... He wanted to die. Well, maybe not *die*. Bad analogy.

"Brice?"

"That was wrong in so many ways."

Jake stiffened beneath him then. "Oh." Blue eyes flitted back and forth. Brice had no idea what was whirling behind them. He wasn't entirely sure he wanted to know, either. He'd embarrassed himself worse than in any way, on any other day, he could remember.

He managed to rise up and Jake let him go. Finding his feet, he braced himself with an outstretched hand on the couch. Worse now, his boner was in plain sight, outlined in his loose pajamas. Mortification times ten.

Jake lurched to his feet and faced Brice without meeting his gaze. "I guess I should be heading home, anyway."

Brice glanced down, away, anywhere but at Jake. "Thank you for being here. You were a huge help."

"Would it be okay if I see how you're doing later in the week?"

Brice snapped his attention to Jake, noticing he was holding out his glasses now. He took them gratefully and slipped them on. "Of course," he replied. "Why wouldn't you?" *Unless...* Oh geez, had he screwed things up that badly? "I mean, we're still friends, right? I didn't..." He was digging himself further, he could feel it. His feet took it upon themselves to try to escape before his mouth could do more damage but Jake snaked a hand out and linked his wrist.

"Brice." A knowing smile began to warm Jake's features, making Brice nervous.

Damn, he's going to tell me to kiss off. I knew it!

What Brice was expecting and what Jake did were so opposite, he was stunned silent.

Jake closed the gap between them and kissed him.

* * * *

Jake was laughing lightly inside. Now he knew what had tied up the sleepy-cute blond he'd held for the last four hours. There was no way that kiss was wrong.

The second one was even better. He'd shocked Brice enough to part his lips and enjoy their heat. He didn't release him, rather using his opposite hand to thread into Brice's short hair and hold on. There *was* gentleness, but there was no question.

Jake was kissing him, *wanted* his kiss, and wasn't letting him go until he understood that.

Brice thought he'd done something wrong. Jake could easily make that guess. He didn't know why, but he could certainly correct the misunderstanding.

He slanted, sipping firmly at Brice's upper lip and the man's body all but melted into him. Brice's moan was rich and long. Jake was careful enough to not hold him too tightly. Brice was getting around better, but there were still flashes of pain and he was moving at a snail's pace to do most things.

Jake released him with a little lick to the tip of his upper lip, catching the fine tremor that rocked Brice when he did, and finding it endearing.

"Still want to say you're sorry?" he teased gruffly, holding Brice in both hands and not letting him go.

"I'm not sure. Should I? Because now I really don't want to."

Brice's dazed smile told Jake more than he was saying openly.

He lifted a hand and spread it across Jake's chest. "That didn't feel like a first kiss, either."

"Trying to get secrets out of *my* closet?" Brice's blush spread. Jake wasn't sure he'd stopped in the last ten minutes. "I'll make you a deal. I'll answer your questions, the next time I see you."

"What's the deal part of it?" Brice asked.

"You have to agree to see me again."

Brice tipped back on his heels. "You... You're not mad about the..."

Jake allowed the bubbling laugh to break free. Blond hair played through his fingers with their movements, but Jake hadn't let him go yet. He wasn't sure if Brice was even aware of the fact that he was still holding him in his hands. "Didn't the second one make that clear? Maybe I should give a third and a fourth while I'm at it." He leaned close enough to grasp at Brice's lower lip with his own, tugging gently.

"But—"

Jake shook his head. "That's one of those secrets and you haven't agreed."

"Of course I'll see you again!" Brice blurted. His lips thinned and lashes lowered in a pain-filled reaction. He drew a slow breath when he could.

Instantly Jake was holding him close, tenderly. "Easy." He looked at the clock. "It's time for the next round of drugs anyway."

Brice lowered his forehead to Jake's shoulder. "Does it sound pathetic that it simply feels nice to have someone care for me, even if it's only for two days and only because some asshole student tried to slice me in two?"

Jake nuzzled Brice's temple. "Not in the least. I do need to go home, but..." He stopped the retreat as soon as he felt Brice's shoulder flex. "I can stay a little longer, and I will be seeing you again."

After a nod of agreement, Jake led Brice with the fingers still clasped around his wrist to the bathroom. Jake checked Brice's sutures and then reapplied gauze. "Gonna have a killer scar," he said, using a light touch to reapply tape. Bruising was prominent across his lower ribs and abdomen but at least he was showing signs of healthy healing. He came too close to worse for Jake's peace of mind.

"I can make up a superhero story to go with it," Brice offered, staring down at Jake's handiwork.

Jake stood next to the bathroom sink and put up the supplies. "Promise me, if you have anything change, you will call someone. And don't try to do too much. You're on bed rest for the next week—" He shook his head when Brice opened his mouth to protest. "—Regardless of how much you think you have to be back in the classroom tomorrow. Trust me, you can't win. You may teach teenagers; I raised one."

That had Brice smiling again. "Okay."

After the bandage change, Jake made lunch because he wanted to, not because Brice couldn't have done it himself. Brice may have missed having someone care for him. Jake missed having someone who appreciated his efforts. Appreciation wasn't exactly Sissy's style. Rebecca did, but it was a different kind of relationship.

With the food ready, he called Brice into the kitchen and instead of just sitting down to eat as Jake expected, he wrapped his arms around Jake from behind and rested his chin on Jake's shoulder. "Smells wonderful. Thank you."

"I have to make sure you eat." He spun gently in Brice's loose hold. "And under no circumstances are you to touch the garden until the doctor releases you. That is non-negotiable."

"Seriously?" Brice blinked owlishly at him from behind his glasses.

"If you pull those sutures, you're back in the hospital for a day."

Brice grumbled, then sighed. "You have a point."

Jake kissed the corner of his mouth. "Food and rest."

"Yes, mother." This time when he said it, Jake laughed deeply, holding Brice close in his arms.

Arms that had long missed doing exactly that.

Chapter Nine

Brice had downgraded to an over-the-counter pain killer by the time he was back in his classroom. And bless his students, they'd been the epitome of angels since his return. No arguing, quick to answer, calm and essentially everything a senior class in last period rarely was.

He wasn't moving at full speed, but he wasn't crawling around any longer either. Being on a week of bed rest had been nerve-racking! Worried about the shenanigans his students would be getting into. Worried about just how much they'd missed or ignored in the week he'd been out.

He'd received a robust round of welcomes and hugs the Monday he'd returned, including three vases of flowers. The reaction to his return to the classroom was one of the few times in his life he would have cried in public, but managed to make it to the teacher's restroom before he couldn't hide it.

He had moved to Jasper because of the job, but it was more than that now. He was really feeling like he'd come home. Brice had a great circle of very supportive friends, and a community that had rallied behind him after the attack.

On top of that, almost every night of the week he'd been at home, Jake had called. Sometimes Rebecca would call to keep him company, picking his brain for her paper, or talking about West Virginia and where he was from. She didn't pry too hard, but she seemed genuinely fascinated by his background and history.

On the nights he spoke to Jake, they'd talked about nearly everything under the sun. Everything from computers to vacations. Brice learned Ian was having a tasting the following weekend to check his own secret rub recipe to prepare for the cook-off. When Brice learned Jake was coming to help, he knew he wouldn't be missing that for anything.

He just had to get through this week. Which meant last period.

He looked at the plain white school clock from where he sat at his desk to check the time, then said, "Okay, class. Don't forget, exams next week. I do recommend brushing up on the Roman eras again. That will be covered. All the Friday chapter tests will be good studying material too." A quiet round of groans was faint, but there. "You know what's going to be covered. It hasn't exactly been a government secret."

That earned a few twitters. Then the bell rang.

"Have a good weekend, Mr. Reynolds," Angela called as she walked by with a smile.

"You too."

A few more said goodbye then he was alone. And he sighed. One more week of classes, then a week of cleaning out the room and end-of-year school board red tape. Then... *Freedom!*

He began to gather up his papers and planner. The sun was bright outside and it was the weekend. He had a garden in desperate need of TLC. He'd neglected it except for the most undemanding tasks. Now that he was on light activity he could at least get his hands dirty again.

"I heard there's a sexy teacher in this room."

Brice whipped around to face the door.

"Jake." He couldn't and didn't try to hide his pleased surprise, smiling goofily. He'd realized during the week of his home stay the drugs really hadn't been the cause of that reaction at all. The smile, the one on his face at exactly that moment, would appear with simply talking to him over the phone. "What are you doing here?"

"You, Ian, then you," he said, purred really as he prowled up to the desk. He drew an apple from behind his hip and placed it on the desk. "Can I be the teacher's pet?"

"Wow." Brice swallowed, feeling flushed all of a sudden. His heart pounded. He swore the temperature in the room shot up a few degrees.

"I like that reaction." Jake slid him a heated look from beneath dark lashes. "Want to get out of here and say it again? Like after I kiss you senseless?" He stopped at the corner of the desk, mere inches from Brice and drifted a fingertip up the top of Brice's hand.

"Thought..." Oh, hell, what did he think? He couldn't think. He was officially mush.

"Thought?" Jake prodded. "I did say you were going to see me again. This weekend just worked in my favor. My brother-in-law said my presence was requested. I know how that was meant. So I have a reason, but honestly, I didn't need one." He leaned close to Brice, not really touching, but the heat of his breath raced past Brice's ear and shot a shiver like a comet down his spine. "Let's get out of here. We can neck under the bleachers."

Brice's eyes flew wide, then he burst out laughing. Jake's smile was wicked, making him oh, so tempting. And unbelievably handsome.

He stuffed the forgotten clutched papers into his shoulder satchel, not even concerned to their state. He slid it over a shoulder. "Where's Rebecca?" He grabbed the apple and polished it on his shirt, saving it.

"With Terra and her uncles."

Walking out of the room, he closed the door, then together they strolled down the hall.

"Bye, Mr. Reynolds."

He smiled and nodded blindly in answer. He only wanted to get out of there as fast as he could. Jake walking next to him as casual as a cat was driving him insane.

"Wow, who's the hottie with Mr. Reynolds?"

A quick glance out of the corner of his eye caught Jake's expression. He'd heard and was biting his lip to not burst out in joined laughter.

Then as if to make it clear, Jake palmed his hand and knitted their fingers together. "This hottie is taken," he murmured through a broad grin.

Brice almost floated all the way to the parking lot. He had no idea what Jake was doing, had even less of an idea of what he was trying to achieve. He still had a list of questions. During all the conversations they'd shared since Jake had returned home, none of them had covered the questions that had been plaguing Brice. It was like a silent, mutual agreement had been made.

They would talk, of that he was sure, but only when they could be together, and unless he was reading this all wrong, that together was also going to be just them...alone.

"Can I kiss you now?" Jake asked quietly once they stood beside his car. The teasing in his voice was gone.

The serious need struck Brice, enflaming him. "In the parking lot?"

"I'll wait if it will cause you problems." Jake lifted a hand and touched his face, staring hard, tracing every line and angle. "These last two weeks surprised me."

"What? How?"

"How much I would want to kiss you, then not liking it when I couldn't." Blue eyes sought his, clear and deep. "I know what you're thinking, or at least wondering. Yes, I will tell you. Let's go to your place. The girls were already into their Friday when I left Rebecca at Caleb's."

Meaning wild laughter and probably ear-splitting squeals as they unwound.

Brice nodded and unlocked his car and slid into it. He couldn't deny the urge and watched Jake stride across the lot to the front of the school to get his own car, and enjoyed the view the entire time. He pulled into his driveway a few minutes later, Jake right behind him.

Brice couldn't help but admire the man from this angle as well as he unfolded from the smart-styled sedan. Today he wore snug jeans, which wrapped around his hips and thighs in black denim and a turquoise blue pullover shirt, opened at the throat. Brice wondered if Jake dressed like that just to make it hard on him to think.

His hips were strong, a flat stomach and chest, and well-muscled arms. Taut with definition. Brice unconsciously licked his lips as wanting unfurled within at his approach.

Jake must have spotted the reaction because blue eyes began to glitter as he drew closer.

"Mmm hmm." Jake hummed in appreciation when he stopped about two feet away. "I'm hot for teacher."

Brice's face roasted with heat. "Jake!"

Jake blinked in sheer devil-born innocence.

There was a natural tease, a sexual draw in his gait that was only confusing Brice further.

Brice shook his head and leaned in slack-jawed confusion against his car. "I don't understand you."

"I can't help it. You look at me in a certain way and I want to beat my chest and howl."

"When did that happen?"

"Honestly? Since the moment I met you, over a year ago. I just had to reacquaint myself with certain facts and truths." He offered a hand. "Come on. Let's go inside."

Stumbling as much literally as mentally, Brice clasped his hand and followed Jake's lead.

Focusing on only one thing at a time to get them into the house without walking dumbly into the door first, he unlocked the door and both went in. Jake slid the satchel free from Brice's shoulder and placed it on the floor.

Brice was still feeling lost, adrift, and confused. They'd shared a few kisses, and some close moments, but this... This was mind-altering lust. Desire that *burned*. Brice was scared to get too close because he didn't know if he'd be fried to a cinder or not. And Jake was making a vivid no-bones about it statement. Only...

"You're straight," Brice choked out. "What are you doing?"

"Not nearly what I want to be doing," Jake answered calmly. He braced an arm beside Brice's head on the door with a flat hand, boxing him in with his body. "Those kisses we shared weren't my first. It's been twenty years since I touched a man." Brice opened his mouth, but Jake made a shushing sound. "Before you say anything, let me get this out."

Brice swallowed, barely daring to breathe.

"I love women. I never doubted that, but I also realized when I was eighteen men were sexy as sin. That when I was looking at other guys, I wasn't just looking, I was *wanting*. Some were beautiful. Some were hunks. Some were assholes. Life happened. Rebecca...*happened*. I do not regret that, her, ever. I regret having a choice as important as who I spend my life with made for me."

Brice slackened against the door, peering into the brightest, most mesmerizing blue eyes before him. Pure truthfulness poured from the man holding him between the prison of those eyes and his arms.

"I'd forgotten what it felt like to touch, forgotten the growl of a man's voice in my ear."

Brice quivered. His eyes slid shut, panting.

"You intrigued me. You are one of the smartest men I've ever run across. You treated Rebecca with so much respect that I wanted to kiss you standing in the garden with handfuls of dirt. Then you were stabbed and my heart stopped. I mean it *stopped*. It felt like I'd had the floor kicked out from under me. But was I still straight? Right then, even I didn't know. I do now."

"Now?" It was a gasped croak.

"Now. It's realizing that what I felt then is still a part of me, that it never changed. Life happened, but that part of me never left, never changed. It was only packed away as unnecessary to life. I was married and never strayed, either. No women...or men."

Jake cupped his jaw with a tender palm. Brice wanted to melt at the simplistic nature of that action.

"I've been thinking since those kisses. And for the first time since Sissy told me she was pregnant, I feel like me. I feel...complete. And even better?"

Brice gulped, gasping a sound, a question, a query that he prayed Jake understood.

"I really like the reason I feel this way again. Does that answer your questions?"

Brice cracked his eyes open to find Jake a hairsbreadth from his lips, wide eyes watching him intently, studying him for any nuance of his thoughts.

"This part, that was forgotten," Brice whispered.

Jake nodded, listening avidly.

"Men. Before..."

"Yes. Men. It was still experimenting to me then. Still...discovering. Then the choice was made for me."

Brice was surprised at the amount of sympathy and empathy welling up for Jake. To be thrown out of sync so early in life when he was just beginning to form his own directions and desires. While Brice may not have been overtly vocal, he hadn't had to forcibly redirect his life because of outside influences. If Jake hadn't taken the path of marriage, had rather decided to pay, had decided something utterly different, Brice wondered where he would be now. Which led to only one question he could ask.

"And now? Are you still attracted to men?"

"To men? I don't know, really. I haven't tried or hunted for possibilities."

It felt like a weight dropped out of the bottom of his world with that answer and Brice sagged. "Oh."

"However, if you ask me if I'm attracted to one man, that I *can* answer."

Chapter Ten

Jake raised his thumb and caressed flushed skin in his palm. Nerves sizzled in answer with the mere touch. Pale as sunlight lashes rose, exposing wary and yet hopeful eyes. "So am I straight? Honestly?" He studied the face, the eyes, the very heartbeat of the man he held. "No. And that one man?" He smiled gently.

Brice's eyes slowly widened, brimmed with heat. Then he did that lip thing, touching it with his tongue and Jake groaned. *That...* That right there. That was the look that drove him insane. Like Brice wanted to strap him down and gobble him up like Thanksgiving dinner.

He restrained the shiver, but only with a Herculean strength.

"Did I explain this well enough? Did I answer your questions? Because if I don't kiss you in the next three seconds, I'm going to beg."

Brice choked out a barked laugh. He straightened against the door, though he didn't push Jake away, merely brought himself level. He raised a hand, pausing a heartbeat before he pushed it into Jake's hair. Jake sighed, sinking into the strength of that hand. Those fingers massaged, then gripped and tugged, startling him as a soft gasp escaped.

Those first kisses on that fateful weekend he'd stayed to help Brice had been gentle, almost exploratory, yet no real demand had been made.

Brice changed that with no warning.

Jake's fingers clawed the door as Brice clutched at him and held him immobile. Jake still leaned into him, still framed his body beneath his own, yet it was Brice who made the next moments happen. Brice sliced a finger beneath the waist of Jake's jeans and tugged, bringing them hip to hip. Not a single gap remained.

The kiss that followed was...heaven. Unbelievable. Passionate. Hard, challenging and hungry. Jake groaned, a deep roar of sound that echoed between his ears. Brice made no bones about claiming full control and Jake had no issues with giving it to him.

The hard thrust of tongue rolled his eyes into his head. They dueled side by side, dancing and chasing each other until Jake had to break for a gulp of air. The hand in his hair tilted him toward the ceiling and Brice licked at him like he was a treat.

"Brice," Jake whined. He wanted to wrap his arms around him and feel skin.

Words escaped him as his world spun. He wasn't ignorant or untutored in passion, but this was blowing his mind. Every nip and lick, suck and nibble shattered him, over and over.

It had been a while since he'd had sex, but that was all it had been: sex. This was...powerful. Blood raced as Brice maneuvered him, inched him this way and that to reach, to find dips and valleys with tongue and teeth. Chills rocked him when he succeeded in finding sensitive spots.

"*Ahh.*"

Brice's laugh rumbled, pleased. "Taste so good," he breathed against Jake's neck. Diving beneath the collar of his shirt, he bit at Jake's collarbone. "Did you have any plans for after that kiss?" Brice asked.

"No," he moaned. He hadn't thought that far ahead. Chest to chest, he was burning. At the moment, he didn't have plans for anything. Maybe breathing. Yeah, that was a good plan. "*Ohh,* Brice." He groaned again, thrusting his hips forward to feel something, anything, more. Clothes were suddenly cumbersome and there were way too many of them. He gathered shirt fabric and slid his hand beneath it, feeling the warmth of Brice's body beneath his palm.

He had to see more. He'd seen Brice while taking care of his wound, but never fully unclothed, and never naked. Now he'd die if he couldn't see him.

He grasped at the shirt, tugging and Brice moved enough to let it flow over his head, then he resumed his attack on Jake's neck and jaw. What the man could do with his tongue... Jake shivered as damp teasing flicked at his earlobe.

Jake opened his eyes and stared at a smorgasbord of silken skin, pale like cream before the warmth of a summer tan. The little rounds of his nipples were a bright rose. He wanted to lick on those so badly. Looking at all that skin, it was natural to seek the scar, to see how he was healing. His gaze fell to it.

Reality struck with a mind numbing chop and he couldn't breathe. It was like seeing the wound for the first time. His world shrank to the single line, a still raw pink with the tight row of sutures in place.

He sank to his knees. Brice didn't fight him. The tight hand in his hair gentled. Jake traced the outer edges lightly with a fingertip. "Still sore?"

"Not so much. Every now and then."

"You're healing okay?"

"The doctor said I was. I think I can believe him," Brice teased with a smile.

Jake nodded, swamped by all the feelings, then and now as they tossed within. He leaned close and pressed his cheek to Brice's stomach. He hadn't been lying. When he'd gotten Caleb's phone call those weeks before, it stunned him like he'd been kicked in the stomach hearing Brice had been injured. He hadn't thought about that reaction other than it had been a friend who'd been hurt.

Now he knew better. He cared about Brice.

Gliding to the side, he grazed light kisses to his abdomen, feeling the way flesh danced and leaped beneath his learning touch. Brice cupped the back of his head, encouraging him, holding him for more. A thin trail of blond hair with a hint of red peeked above his waistline. He swept a broad stroke across the flat expanse in front of him with his tongue, reveling in the texture, the firmness, the taste.

In his youth, he'd been with guys, though it wasn't like this. There had always been one goal, for the both of them, and this kind of sense-driven enjoyment hadn't been it.

A soft hiss floated down to him and he smiled. He loved how his caresses were affecting Brice.

"Jake, before you get too much further, can we move away from the door?"

He raised to his feet in front of Brice and this time commanded the kiss. He would have shouted in sheer pleasure when he felt Brice go boneless this time because of it. Only his mouth was otherwise occupied.

Panting, he drew away. Then, like he'd been doing all along, he clasped a hand and urged Brice to follow. He went straight to the bedroom. It didn't matter what they did. All that mattered was he was holding Brice, and for the first time in a very long time, he was happy. He wasn't sure what he wanted, wasn't sure where to go next. But he was happy.

Then Brice moved against him, angling for a kiss and Jake gave it to him. He cradled his head in both hands and devoured him. He felt Brice's hands on his chest, and shuddered beneath their questing. He slid a hand down and grasped at his wrists. "No, let me."

Brice blinked green pools and slowly relaxed.

He slipped Brice's glasses off and sidestepped to place them on the nightstand. "I want to discover you."

A shuddering breath shook Brice as he patiently waited.

Jake ran his hands from Brice's shoulders, down his chest, lightly scraping over the pointed tips of flesh that begged for touch. Brice shivered, little goose bumps rising in his wake. "So sweet," Jake murmured, watching the way his body leaned for more, hungered for more.

Brice's lips were gently parted, plump from all their kisses. Heavy-lidded eyes watched him while his hands hung at his sides, flexing into fists over and over. He was giving Jake freedom to explore.

Jake was loving it. He sank to the floor in front of him again, determined fingers undoing the belt in his pants and sliding it free to reach the button beneath. Then the zipper. Jake leaned close, inhaling to capture the raw musk of aroused male flesh. His heart pounded. Fingers threaded into his hair and his shoulders clenched in response. Firm but not demanding. Guiding but not forceful.

This was so different from touching a woman. He knew it, but even after Sissy left, he'd only sought out women. Was it because he was comfortable? Knew what was expected? Knew there would be no demands? Why had there been no men to draw his eye? Why hadn't the dormant need reawakened as soon as he'd been free? Jake didn't know, and couldn't answer the questions dancing through his mind.

A quiet sigh reached his ears. Jake closed the miniscule gap and stroked the telling ridge behind cotton with the flat of his tongue. The fingers holding him tightened. Jake ate up the way Brice's body twitched.

Jake let his desires dictate his next move, and the only thing he knew was he desperately wanted to taste the man in front of him. The paleness of Brice's skin drew him. Called to him like a lover's sweet enticement.

The band of underwear rolled low and Brice's body lay in plain sight. Jake whined quietly in his throat. Smooth as satin, the tip peeked at him from the hood of skin protecting him. Translucent and blushed pink as blood pulsed to fill the entire shaft. Jake swallowed. Longing and daring collided, pushing him to take the plunge, one he willingly wanted to fulfill. The weight was heady on his tongue, the taste an elixir that sent blood coursing through his veins. The reaction was so intense, he gasped.

"Oh, God, Jake." Brice held him, a hand over his ear, the other lost in his hair.

The next thing he did simply happened. He drew the length he held on his tongue deep and held him there. Panted breathing was the best he could do as his heart raced with excitement. Gazing upward, he clashed with heavy green eyes watching him as well.

"That is so sexy," Brice whispered.

Lashes fluttered when Jake undulated his tongue against the vein on the underside of Brice's hard shaft. Jake closed his own eyes then and enjoyed himself, sucking and licking, loving everything about it, from the heat between his lips to the caress and strength of the hands that held him.

This was actually something he'd only done one time before and that had been in the backseat of a car behind a club, yet with Brice it felt wholly natural. There was nothing clandestine in his motions or desires. Forgotten sensations and memories were rekindled. Desires flared into being. With braced palms anchored on Brice's hips, he lost himself to the act, to the thrill of feeling smooth skin glide between his lips and teeth. The slight bitter-sweet taste of Brice's excitement added to the fire already in his blood. When Brice strained against him, Jake moaned.

Leaning forward he choked unexpectedly and quickly slipped to the end, gasping as he fought the reflex to let go completely.

Brice's concern was clear in the absolute stillness in his frame. Then there was a light sweep of fingers over Jake's ear, comforting.

"Are you okay there? I do have a bed." Brice's voice was lightly cajoling.

"Next time," Jake stated. He was fine and he wasn't moving. He didn't want to stop for the time it would take to move. With closed lips, he grazed the smooth tip twice against the seam, then opened up to gorge himself.

Raising a hand to the thickness he was adoring, he built up speed, gliding in a rocking up and down motion that simply felt perfect. Tingles sparked beneath skin. Desire and craving surged into a burn that demanded fulfillment. Hearing Brice's gasps turning into wisped moans encouraged him more than anything he'd ever experienced.

"Jake. *Jaaake*," he cried.

Yes! God, Brice, give it to me. Jake couldn't speak for what he wanted, instead he pleaded with his touch, gripping and pumping in blatant encouragement. Within heartbeats, Brice's cock pulsed. The first jet was a hot shock, then he sucked like a Las Vegas hooker and drained Brice until he was trembling. The hand that had gripped his hair, clung for balance.

Carefully he released Brice, licking the pulsing flesh to capture the last drops, holding Brice steady as his legs wobbled. Brice's entire upper body was flushed, his chest staggering in the need for air.

Jake carefully found his feet in front of the blond. "Come here." He slipped an arm around Brice's waist and drew him close. Brice practically sagged into his strength, melted in the best possible way. Jake smiled, pressing his smile into Brice's neck.

"Now, let's see about that bed," he offered.

Brice nodded. "Bed, yes."

Jake chuckled warmly, aware he was well on his way to adoring the man he held.

Chapter Eleven

Jake gazed at the face of the man sleeping next to him in the bed. Light blond hair now stood roughly spiked and in utter disarray from sleep, not to mention the work of hungry hands that couldn't get enough of the texture. In sleep, translucent lashes fanned beneath his eyelids. He knew the color of those eyes, every detail, just by closing his own.

The sun was setting, stretching shadows through the bedroom, yet he was too comfortable to think about disturbing either of them to do something about the time of evening. As far as he was concerned, the world could just spin. He was perfectly happy where he was.

A cautious hand rose and lightly traced the ridge of Brice's nose. Those freckles. They weren't bright, or obvious, but they were adorable. They drew him with the same inquisitive curiosity that a starry sky would demand it be counted. He could try, but he'd never actually succeed. Broadening his exploration, he glided to the gently parted lips; such a lush pink. He could remember, quite easily, their deepened color after a kiss.

It finally struck him why he was so enamored by Brice's natural beauty, because there *was* beauty in his features. The fact was that all of it, all of Brice, was incredibly natural. There was no makeup, no powder, no gloss or lipstick to heighten the fullness or the color of those lips. It would have been a travesty to cover all his natural brilliance—if he'd been a woman.

Sissy had been elegant with her beauty, yet she didn't have this naturalness to her appeal either. After being together almost ten years, and unequivocally in the same bed, Jake couldn't remember once doing what he was doing right then with Brice.

So many years lost. Not wasted, just...already gone. With Sissy and since. He refused to blame, but it was time he wouldn't ever have again. He didn't believe in much, but he did have to believe there was a purpose for every soul, for every individual.

He'd cared for Sissy, and it had fallen apart when he wasn't looking. Or maybe it had never been right to begin with. Wondering over that conundrum was pointless. She was gone, and had been for nearly as long as they'd been together.

Jake had changed over the last two decades. He couldn't truthfully say that Brice would have been the type he would have chased when he was younger. What he wanted in a person had changed. Now? He wanted to do a whole lot more than just chase Brice. He hadn't lied when Brice had asked when all this new enlightenment had occurred. He had been completely attracted to Brice at Caleb's wedding. Only... Jake had avoided it, still refusing to unpack those long ago needs and desires. He'd put them away when his life's course had been decided. He'd thought they were gone, done, unneeded and he'd lived day to day, raising Rebecca and doing his job. If he found another woman who appealed to him enough to draw on his emotions, then so be it. He had been on dates, but not much else. He hadn't thought of men on a personally intimate level because he hadn't thought of *anyone* in that way.

Then he'd had the chance to get to really know Brice, to call him a friend and it didn't matter whether Jake thought he was done with those needs or not.

Brice brought them out and made Jake hungry for all the things he'd put behind him.

Jake's sex life had been sparse but not an utter void. He knew what he liked in women. Knew a firm ass and soft peaked nipples on rounded, medium-sized tits could turn his head faster than a slingshot. The bigger the better rule had never applied to him. He used to love wet T-shirt contests. He liked a woman who was confident, assured and compassionate. Smarts was a plus. He hated talking over a person's head. If they played the *I'm stupid* card, no woman got more than a hello from him.

Then came Brice... He sighed quietly, focusing in front of him and the man behind his careening thoughts.

Jake was still an ass man. No matter how he sliced it. He'd have to lie to say he hadn't noticed Brice's. Perfectly round and high. It was made for love bites. Instead of breasts, he loved the paleness of his skin. He didn't even have tan lines. Jake was sure he'd burn to a crisp if he were outside for too long.

So, no long, dark hair, rather playfully spiked and sunlight blond. No breasts, instead a strong chest that sloped into an amazingly tempting stomach, and even without the perkiness that a woman would have, Jake had sucked on the flushed, hardened nubs like he wanted to drive both of them out of their minds. He'd succeeded.

There was a rich musk to Brice that made Jake's mouth water and his heart pound. There were also the contrasts. The hints of red, the beautiful green of his eyes. The lush pink of his lips against all that cream skin.

When he'd first felt attraction for Brice, he'd thought he could ignore it, thought it was exaggerated and unnecessary.

How wrong he'd been. It was only growing stronger as he found out more about the man, learned the little facets that made him a person, a teacher, a listener, and now, a lover. Fingertips coasted north to wind through strands of wayward hair. Brice had definition a woman simply couldn't. There was something in both men and women that had always drawn Jake's eye. Like Caleb had said, an aesthetic quality. The curve of a shoulder, the dip of a waist and the smooth flow of a hip.

He'd positively enjoyed exploring Brice's frame, all the curves and angles, contours and muscles. He drifted his hand over the shell of Brice's ear, coasting down to his jaw. When he raised his eyes, he landed on green orbs gazing back at him.

Jake surged forward slowly, until he was even with Brice's lips. Curiosity watched him with an unblinking fascination.

Gliding an arm beneath Brice's body, he rolled the other man into him. Brice let him, not fighting the invitation. Then Jake began to nibble on Brice's jaw, the curve from chin to ear. A low, raw sigh filled the quiet and Brice went pliant in his arms.

They were both naked, which made it sinfully delicious to feel skin glide against skin as each shifted, as each breathed. Brice edged himself up onto his elbows to stare down at Jake. Lashes danced as Jake continued his languid roaming, licking and tasting over Brice's jaw and neck. He purred when he latched onto Brice's pulse point. Brice's full body shudder was impossible to miss.

"Mmm," Jake murmured, licking over the same spot he'd just worried. "Don't want to mark you, but it is so tempting."

"A hickey?"

Jake nuzzled upward, caressing with his nose and lips. "Yeah. It turns me on just thinking about it. This canvas of skin with my mark on you." He swept a lazy palm from beneath Brice's jaw to his throat and down between his collar bones. The contrast even between the two of them was striking to see, and Jake loved it. "You've never seen the inside of a tanning booth, have you?"

"No." He raised a fraction, a glimpse of distress in his look. "Is that bad?"

"Hell no," Jake chuckled, smiling upward until Brice relaxed. "I'd rather this than over baked and overdone." He rubbed circles with a thumb over a collar bone.

"I've always thought I was too pale, too white," Brice told him.

Jake tipped his head on the pillow to find Brice's gaze. "Not too pale, and I've never heard of being too white." He scoffed.

Brice braced himself on a planted elbow above Jake. Chest to chest. "Comfortable?" Jake asked, noting how Brice was avoiding the left side of his ribs.

"Enough," he replied. He trailed fingertips down Jake's sternum. "What's your curfew?"

"Do I have to leave?" Jake countered. He splayed a hand in the dip of Brice's spine, keeping him near.

"I won't kick you out, but I understand if you're expected somewhere." Brice tipped his head on his neck, resting at an angle to study Jake.

"I would just be going to Caleb's to sleep. Personally, I like this bed a lot more."

Brice's lips twitched in return to Jake's playfulness. "Oh?"

"No question. It has you in it."

Brice's face warmed with that delicious red that Jake adored. *So damned cute.* Jake doubted Brice even suspected his thoughts.

He stroked the body he held in his arms. Honestly, if he didn't have to get out of bed the entire weekend, he'd be fine. Discovering Brice, reawakening the needs that the other man stoked innocently was infinitely more enticing than anything else Jake could name. That would even include Ian's call to arms over the barbecue, only that would be one he'd never live down if he skirted his duty to his brother-in-law. At least Brice was invited too, and had offered his help for the cook-off.

Brice purred quietly, in time with Jake's slow petting. Kissing his neck, he urged Brice over, laying him on his back until Jake rested above him. Then he adored Brice in earnest.

Chapter Twelve

Jake took his time, a lingering kiss to sweet lips before they got out of the car. He couldn't help but feel a thrill at Brice's languid recovery when they parted. Hazy eyes, slow movements, and a sweet smile. The newness of what he shared with Brice was sinking in. He wasn't about to rush into anything, not after sacrificing a decade to Sissy, and then being responsible for Rebecca. He was going to take his time. He was going to enjoy this, and see where it took him. He liked Brice. A lot. But whether it was fascination, the unknown, or just being wanted again, he was going to take this a step at a time.

For all he knew, now that his desires had been brought out of cold storage, the love of his life might be right around the corner. He wasn't going to play this game blindly. Not this time around. He was also perfectly aware the person beside him was someone special, and no less aware that Brice was male.

Jake latched onto Brice's lingering gaze and smiled. "One more."

Simmering heat lit Brice's eyes as they neared and kissed, then Jake closed his eyes and simply felt the want. The warmth of lips. The tease of skin. He whimpered once, wanting more, wanting to back the car away from the house and find a quiet place to get down to skin.

Brice's calloused palm caressed his cheek. With a slow sip and regretting the need, they separated.

"Wonder if they'd miss us?" Jake asked.

Redness ghosted over Brice's cheekbones. "Out. Or I'm going to kiss you again."

"That's not a threat," Jake replied.

Brice leaned close and touched mouth to mouth, then reluctantly sat straight. Both moved to get out of the car and when he glanced up, Jake's heart froze.

Standing yards in front of the car was Rebecca, staring directly into it. Unmoving.

"Uh oh," Brice whispered. "Are you in trouble?"

"I don't know."

In unison, they opened doors and stood beside the car. Jake swiveled to look at Brice over the vehicle. "Go ahead. I'll be right there."

Brice's worried gaze flickered between them, then he nodded.

"Hello, Rebecca," Brice offered as he passed her. She barely moved, staring openly at her dad. There were a lot of questions in that blank expression. He sincerely hoped he had the right answers to give her.

Jake walked to the front of the car and rested on the fender. "Come talk to me," he encouraged, patting the curve beside him. He crossed his arms over his chest and waited.

Stiffly, she approached then gingerly leaned on the car at his shoulder.

"Ask whatever is on your mind," he told her.

It took a few minutes but eventually she did. "Is that where you stayed last night?"

"Yes, and I'll probably be there again tonight. Love Caleb and Ian, but they only have one spare bed."

"And he has a spare bed?" she challenged.

Jake stifled the sigh. It didn't sound like she was jealous, just trying to come to terms, with a mere hint of teenager mad and angst for color. He knew it could have been so much worse.

"Technically, yes." Well, he *did* have a couch, Jake mused.

She lifted dark eyes. "Except, *technically* you're not using it, right?"

He shook his head.

"So, are you dating him?"

"I'm not sure what we have yet. Being bi isn't something I've thought about in almost twenty years." The words were a lot easier to say than he would've thought. Maybe he was closer to accepting for himself, too. All he knew was he didn't want to hurt his baby girl.

"Bi? Bi-sexual?" She choked on the words. Her head sagged backward, her eyes staring unseeing upward. "Wow. My dad is bi-sexual."

"Is it really that bad?"

"No." She straightened enough to mimic him with the crossed arms, slouched against the car. "Not really. Just trying to wrap my head around it." She kicked a foot over an ankle and rolled a shoulder. "I'm not used to seeing you with anyone, other than Mom and since that hasn't happened in ages..."

He studied her. "I see. It's me with someone, not that Brice is a guy."

"Well, actually, yes that Brice is a guy matters, but when it feels like it should be the priority issue, it really isn't coming in first."

That was a relief for Jake. It wasn't that he hadn't thought about telling Rebecca, but he hadn't really considered when he would say anything, or how he would go about explaining it. Springing it on her less than twenty-four hours after he'd proven his intentions to Brice hadn't been one of his planned options. He wasn't sure where he stood fully with Brice, so he was hesitant to cause more upheaval for her by making premature claims or creating false illusions about their relationship.

He wasn't going to hurt her, or get her hopes up if all this was between himself and Brice was incredible sex and a really deep sense of like.

"Are you okay if we see where this goes?" he asked her.

She didn't look up from her wiggling toes in her sandals. "It's not like I'm going to throw a tantrum, that you can't have someone in your life." She paused. "It's just weird. He lives here, he's a guy, and a friend."

He took his time to answer her points. They were valid and she deserved the truth. "The first means we have to plan a little, that this isn't going to be a weekend fling. Being a friend? I'm glad you still see him that way. He doesn't want to hurt you either." Jake reached and pushed a wave of hair away from his daughter's face. *As for the guy factor?* "I know it'll take time to become comfortable."

"I'm okay with Uncle Caleb and Ian."

"I know you are, honey. But I'm not them, and it's going to feel strange and look even more so with Brice and me." He put an arm around her shoulders and tucked her into his chest. "No matter what, I'll always be your dad and you'll always come first."

"Does Mom know?"

"No. I stopped everything when she became pregnant with you. I'd dated girls since I was sixteen, and a few guys when I got to college. I hadn't thought about men, or had it cross my mind until Caleb's wedding to Ian." He nuzzled into her with his chin, stroking her spine with a thumb. "I saw him and felt the world shift that day. It was so unexpected."

"Really bi, huh?" She gave him a quirked glance.

"Really bi. Some of us just take a little longer to come around."

She laughed gently. Finally she said, "I want you to be happy. Mom got what she wanted." Rebecca tipped to stare up into his face. "Your turn."

Jake examined her expression and almost squeezed the stuffing out of her, but managed to tame it to a hard hug. "Thanks, honey."

He slid an arm around her waist and they walked together to the backyard to join the rest of Ian's guinea pigs.

* * * *

Brice tried to hide the anxiousness roiling within with smiles and laughter, but when neither Jake nor Rebecca followed him around the house for several minutes, he couldn't stem the worry. Indecision knifed him. Should he stay? What was going to happen now? Did anyone in Jake's family know why, exactly, he'd stayed last night at Brice's? Did they suspect? Would they be okay with it?

Just then, Caleb walked up behind Ian who was manning the grill and whispered in his ear, a flash of a secretive smile and lowered lashes giving away all too much information. Caleb's family embraced them. Would they do the same for Jake? Brice realized this, what they were both trying to build on, was a strong left turn no one in his family will be expecting.

Would it cost Brice his friends? What about Rebecca? He sincerely did not want to hurt her.

"Hey," Jake breathed by his ear.

So lost in thought, Brice hadn't heard him at all. He blinked at the other man with wide eyes. "Well?"

"We have her approval," he replied.

Brice sagged in his sneakers, a small tremor rocking him. "Thank God. And the others?"

He shrugged. "I guess we'll find out. I'm sure they are well aware of where I was last night, and that I didn't come here to sleep."

Jake was smiling warmly and Brice really wanted to believe in that look.

"So? Are we dating?" Brice asked, sorry he sounded as hesitant as he did, but he couldn't help the knots.

"Want to give it a shot?"

"Hell yes," Brice returned with enthusiasm.

Jake chuckled and none-too-discreetly reached behind him to slide a hand into Brice's rear shorts pocket, palming flesh with a teasing squeeze. "Let's get something to drink. I'm sure Caleb has tea and beer here somewhere."

"In the house," Ian called as they approached the grill and the other two men. Ian swept a look over them, an arched eyebrow seeming to be the extent of his opinion. "I hope you guys are hungry. I have two trials for today."

Jake rubbed his stomach. "I'm up to it. Is Jessie coming?"

"Not today. A brief he had to finish for a Monday deadline," Caleb answered. "He is working the cases he has so he can be here the whole weekend of the competition."

"How do you feel so far Ian?" Brice asked.

"Pretty good. I tweaked the rubs I used for the chicken, so I'll need you guys to tell me which is the better of the two." He poked at the fire, checking temperatures and the timer, then shut the lid. "Let's go grab a beer."

Caleb walked with Ian, with Brice and Jake trailing them into the house.

Drinks were passed around and they talked for a bit in the kitchen until it was time for Ian to go check the cooking again. Caleb stayed in the kitchen.

"Is Rebecca okay with you two?" Caleb asked, swinging his beer side to side to indicate both Brice and Jake.

"She gave her approval," Jake told him, sharing a soft smile with Brice that knocked his heart into his ribs. Jake was not shy about showing his feelings in front of his brother, and it not only surprised him, it made him feel lightheaded.

"How do you think Sissy will take it?"

Brice felt a tense spasm in Jake that passed quickly. "Don't know, and not sure I really care. Since our divorce, she's been engaged twice and is still playing like she's twenty."

"Wow. You haven't been divorced that long, have you?" Brice couldn't understand that kind of immaturity. Probably because he was faced with real immaturity daily at school, but a large percentage of those simply hadn't been out of their comfort zones to be allowed to mature.

"Eight years, almost nine now." Jake took a healthy swallow of his beer. "We're less than a year apart in age. She also dropped out of school when she became pregnant, and has shown no interest in doing anything about it. At least I didn't have to pay alimony. She got a settlement in the divorce and that was it."

"She sounds like a piece of work."

"I'll have to tell you the rest. It's a story deserving of Jack *and* Jose."

Brice laughed, shaking his head in sympathy. He didn't fight it when the arm wrapped around his waist urged him closer and he leaned willingly into Jake's side.

Chapter Thirteen

"Dad." Rebecca sighed with humor. "You're pacing again."

Jake swiveled to stare at his daughter, then smiled and relaxed. "I know. I can't help it." It had been months since he'd been on a date, and too many years to want to admit to since he'd gone anywhere with a guy.

A horn honked outside. "Oh! That's Deena."

She jumped forward but was halted by a stern warning from Jake.

"Remember. Midnight. You're not eighteen so I know you can't get into too much trouble." *Yet.*

She gave him a quick kiss on the cheek. "I'll be good. It's just a movie." She double checked her pockets. Nothing too outrageous for clothing. Jeans and a trendy blouse, not even a lot of makeup. He guessed her own mother had killed any joy she would have found in it. Jake was grateful his daughter had common sense as well as book sense.

"I know you will," he said.

She popped open the door and waved outside, then said over her shoulder, "Your date is pulling up." She winked broadly and then dashed outside.

Jake walked to the door and propped it open behind her dash to the curb, watching as the two cars swapped places. Deena pulled away and let Brice take her place. The man looked good with the sunset behind him when he got out of the car. Brice waved at Rebecca when they honked then turned that beaming smile on Jake.

Heat flashed through his veins. He hungered for a kiss that he'd been waiting a long week to get. He'd hated having to leave Brice behind on Sunday. Jake had hated leaving period.

He'd stood at Brice's door for more than twenty minutes storing as many kisses as he could before he left for Caleb's to pick up Rebecca and say his goodbyes and thank yous for letting her stay with them.

In crisp slacks and a pullover, the man approaching was this side of GQ hot with his hair spiked just right and those too-smart-for-you glasses. Brice was a walking geek-gasm.

"Hi," he breathed when Brice stopped in front of him.

"Hi yourself." And that grin grew by miles.

"Oh, man. Get in here." He reached, found something to latch onto and tugged Brice through the doorway right into his arms.

Laughter was quickly silenced into quiet moans as Jake devoured him with a hungry kiss that burned. Brice welcomed him when Jake tapped at his lips with the tip of his tongue. The little noises Brice made thrilled him like a brisk winter wind on skin, shivers chasing up and down his frame.

Both were panting when they split. "The drive was okay?"

"Not bad at all. And school is officially out!"

"No more teacher's dirty looks?" Jake tapped a rhythm with a finger on Brice's hip.

Green eyes sparkled behind thin shields of glass. "Not for a few months anyway. Just got to pack up and that will only take a few days to clean out the room, and finish grades."

"Well, are you ready?" Jake was almost bouncing on his toes. He had an evening to remember planned for this guy.

"Whenever you are."

Jake slid one of Brice's hands into his and urged him back out the front door. "Then let's get the night going."

Jake knew exactly where he was starting, and by Brice's grin knew he'd scored when he parked in front of the family-owned Greek restaurant. "Thought you might like a change of pace."

"Nothing even close to this in Jasper."

"And they use all fresh ingredients. They even get their dairy from a local farm, cheese included."

"Wow!" Brice breathed, fully impressed. "I can't remember the last time I had spanakopita."

"You're going to love this one. The beef souvlaki is unbelievable."

"I'm drooling," Brice joked, running a hand over his chin.

Jake bumped his shoulder as they walked to the front door. When they were greeted, Jake asked for a small table near the back, close to the grill. The aromas and scents rising from the cooking made his mouth water like a faucet. It had been too long since he'd been there.

Drink orders were made and they were left alone for a bit to study the menus.

"I wish I could try one of everything. It's been so long since I had this kind of a treat."

"Where did you go to school?" Jake knew he was getting the beef, so he closed his menu and set it by his plate.

"West Virginia University. I have degrees in world history and secondary education, and then applied for a teacher's certificate. My high school teachers were the largest influence on me, and I wanted to give what they'd given me."

"Wow." Jake leaned forward, sharing a mischievous grin. "I think after Caleb and Jessie, my teachers were glad to just get rid of me."

"Trouble makers? I can't imagine," Brice said with a hinted at smirk.

"If you only knew."

"Good evening, gentlemen. Ready to order?"

They made their orders and passed over the menus. Jake was almost bouncing on his chair. He wanted to tackle Brice and kiss him breathless.

And he was pretty sure Brice knew this and was chuckling at him. Jake shrugged. "Can't help it," he murmured. "Missed you all week."

Brice slid a hand across the table and squeezed Jake's. "Missed you too."

That acknowledgement helped calm Jake and he relaxed, flowing into the conversation, enjoying the meal and then the evening as it closed in around them.

When they were almost done, Jake made one last order for dessert, and two drinks to go.

"Oh?" Brice asked.

"Surprise number two."

The heated look Jake received made his pulse dance in answer.

With the container and drinks in hand, Jake led Brice to the car and pulled away from the restaurant.

"Any hints?" Brice looked in his direction, but he just shook his head.

"You'll see."

Brice settled a hand on Jake's thigh, trusting.

In truth, Brice's little touches were killing him. He wanted to make love to the cute blond so badly. They hadn't *quite* gone that far last weekend and Brice hadn't complained. He had let Jake move at his own speed. Now, Jake was nearly bursting with the need to feel all of Brice, to caress and please in a way that would make Brice his first.

In truth, that was partially the cause for his high-energy nerves. This was like wooing his first date all over again, with the hope of getting to third base. *Or home plate.*

Brice sat up a little when Jake pulled into the line behind other cars. He reached for his wallet and paid the cost at the booth, rolling up the window again to keep out the free-flying dust, trailing traffic to grab a decent viewing spot.

Brice had a hand over his mouth, hiding his snickers, watching as people jockeyed for position then settled and turned off cars.

Jake stopped between two audio bars and rolled down the window to reach for the sound box to clip to the window then rolled it up. He cracked the rear windows about half way then turned off the car.

"Surprise number two," he said, with a hand sweep out the windshield.

"I love it! I haven't been to a drive-in since I was a kid."

"Is the movie a good choice?"

"Movie? Who cares! We get to make out in the car!" He doubled over with laughter.

Jake laughed with him, then reached behind the seat to grab the folded blanket he'd dropped back there earlier in the day. He slid the driver's seat all the way back and patted the padded console. "Get comfy. We have dessert to share."

Jake twisted and got comfortable, letting Brice settle between his legs on the seat to hold the man against his chest.

"We'll save the blanket for a little later. It'll cool off without us noticing it." He stuffed it onto the dash, out of the way. Brice's sigh of contentment was music.

"I feel sixteen again."

Jake nuzzled his ear, thrilling at the gentle tremor that rocked Brice. With arms wrapped around him, he threaded their fingers together, hugging him close. "If you get stiff, let me know and we'll move to the backseat."

"Oh, the double *entendre* in that," Brice cooed.

"It wasn't an accident." Jake used his tongue to play with the earlobe by his lips.

Brice snorted through his laughter. Music started to blare through the speaker and they settled in to watch the double feature.

In one way, it was heaven. Jake had Brice all to himself, snuggled tighter than a five year-old to their sleeping bear. Body warmth was just enough to be comfortable. Gentle hand squeezes were sweet and teasing at the same time. Yet, there was the hint of things to come, the press of a hip into Jake's groin, the caress of lips and fingertips as they fed each other the baklava Jake had ordered.

When it was gone, it was a game of seduction to suck the honeyed sweetness off fingers. Then lips.

"Care to switch?" Brice asked with a burr of promise.

"Go ahead. Let me drop the seat forward so we can still see."

Brice's lips twitched. "Uh huh. See." He scrambled, bent and crawled into the backseat, mimicking Jake's prior position deep in the corner.

Jake turned up the volume a couple of notches then squirmed between the seats to join him.

Adjusting the seats took some gymnastics, but soon they had room and were able to see forward. Trading places was fine with Jake. He loved having Brice's touch all over him.

Jake grabbed the blanket before he was fully settled and whipped it open to tuck around them.

"Hmm. Daring to be naughty?" Brice asked, the whispered words deep and sexy.

"More hoping you won't hesitate."

Brice's chest rocked beneath him.

"Watch the movie, flirt."

Anticipation was winding Jake tighter than a windmill in a cyclone. Slow circles singed as Brice petted his chest and stomach. Soon, he unbuttoned Jake's shirt and danced fingertips beneath the edges.

"Hot," Brice bit out with a groan. Jake wiggled, silently asking—begging—for more. "Sexy as sin with this over the muscle shirt. Bad boy."

Jake's eyes closed as sensory overload swamped him. Brice glided fingers down his chest to the button of his jeans. A light tug had it undone. He clutched at Brice's thighs, willing him to go on.

The warmth of a palm skated over fabric, pressing into the erection he'd been cursed with for the last two hours. Not that he was complaining. Not after holding Brice for most of the night, sucking on sugary fingers and nibbling on ears and neck just to hear the sweetest moans and gasps come from the other man.

He guessed he was about to pay for all of that.

He rested his head on Brice's shoulder, surrendering to the uninhibited exploration of that particular hand.

"Having you like this is such a turn on," Brice said quietly, ghosting kisses to Jake's temple.

Jake had lost total interest in the movie now. His heart tripped and pounded as Brice delved and played, inching his way beneath the jeans zipper, slowly letting it grate downward as he burrowed deeper and deeper.

Then Brice wrapped strong but gentle fingers around his shaft and he shuddered.

"Raise your hips."

Jake did and Brice scooted his jeans below his ass and down his thighs. He was grateful the blanket covered him, but he wasn't sure he'd care even if it didn't.

Brice hooked one of Jake's legs over his outer knee and captured his other, effectively sprawling him.

"Wish I could see how you looked right now. Get you naked and spread to four corners."

Jake whined with need. "Killing me, Brice."

Brice shimmied downward a little, bracing Jake while broadening his straddle. "You have no idea how many times I replayed last weekend, your hands all over me. Drove me nuts."

Jake's guffaw was staggered and raw. "I think I might."

Brice's hands were now stroking and touching everywhere, bunching up the thin cotton of his undershirt to reach Jake's nipples and bare chest with questing fingernails. Every single motion was hidden from sight but very far from private. It added another element of risk to each second.

Jake's spine arched as sensation sliced through him. Then Brice's touch was lowering...lowering...

"Oh shit!" He cried out and Brice slid his free hand upward and popped a finger between his lips.

"Shh. Can't have the little ones hearing your orgasm."

Jake rolled his head, following Brice's lead and sucked on the offered finger, imagining it was Brice's dick.

Chapter Fourteen

Brice cupped Jake's sac and teased him with daring fingers. Tremors rocked Brice where they pressed together. Slowly his hand stuttered to a stop, his brain finally registering what his fingers had already known.

"What did you do?" he whispered. He swept his thumb up and around, beneath and over. "You got waxed? When did you do that?"

"Tuesday," Jake mumbled, refusing to release the silencer in his mouth.

"Fucking hell, Jake." Brice groaned, not just a sound of hunger and desire, thrilled with Jake's initiative, but a deep and needy craving that flipped his world. He sank to Jake's shoulder, biting at skin, and not being exactly gentle. "You are making me insane."

A hard suck on his finger seemed to express Jake's agreement.

"All right. You asked for it," he growled.

"I'm begging," he whimpered plainly, wiggling his hips.

Brice stroked the shaft that had to be standing in rapt need beneath the blanket by the poked tent Jake was creating. Hot flesh burned his palm when he clasped Jake's cock. A keening whimper floated between them. The way Jake was rubbing against Brice's front and crotch excited every nerve. "Could slide into you right now. Been wanting to for weeks."

"Don't have... Oh *gawwd*," Jake moaned when Brice pumped his length with powerful strokes. He fell silent with gasps of pleasure breaking that quiet.

Brice reinforced the spread of Jake's legs. There was a good chance he was going to lose it too with the way Jake was pressed into him, as hot as Brice was getting. He shifted, trying to alleviate even the slightest pressure, but it didn't help.

Jake was drawing harder on the digit in his mouth while fingers clawed into Brice's thighs. Jake rocked with each hard stroke of Brice's fist, up and down, twisting and tugging. Velvet skin slipped and glided through his hold. It was a powerful feeling, knowing he was in absolute control of Jake's pleasure, that it would be his choice when he finally found release.

He rolled the knob into the curve of his palm then dropped down again to tease at the smooth skin of his sac. Flesh pulsed. Dewy drops slipped from the slit and helped ease each pass. A telling shiver shook Jake and he moaned.

"That close, huh?" he breathed right into Jake's ear.

A muffled hum for an answer was the most he was going to get apparently. It was heaven touching him, pleasing him, and knowing he was drowning in the sensations. Skin to skin. Body to body. Need and craving were coiling, ready to snap. The telltale signs vibrated throughout Jake's body.

"You treated me so good last weekend. Let me do this. Take what you need, sweetheart," he purred. Brice reached and dared to tease at his opening, feeling a full tremor rock his frame at the same time. Brice loved teasing Jake's body, daring to push, applying pressure. A growled whine filled his ear and he returned to the stroking he'd been in the middle of. Jake was officially in meltdown.

Jake gasped, crying out softly as he lost it. Fingers dug through clothing and held on as Jake's hips thrust through the cage of Brice's fist. Warmth pooled and spread over skin, tugs and squeezes keeping pace with low grunts and pants. The thick scent of semen filled the backseat and Brice moaned.

He rested his forehead against Jake's temple. "Want you naked so bad."

Jake gulped, a dry swallow. "Me too."

A few minutes later, Jake inched upward to adjust his position, his face scrunching up. "I need a shower."

"Want to try to sneak out?"

"Let's go to the stand to wash up. Should be able to leave a little less obviously by then. I think it's almost over." Though by the sluggish speed Jake was moving he wasn't necessarily in a hurry to change their positions or to leave.

Brice wrapped an arm around Jake's shoulder and curled them together. "That was amazing. I like going to the movies with you."

Jake smiled and kissed him right back.

After a languid cuddle, they both went to the concessions stand to use the restroom to wash up, Brice walking a little gingerly. He was still aching in his own pants, stiff and sensitive, though able to let it go, knowing they'd both enjoyed what they'd just shared. He was also confident they weren't done for the night. Jake folded the blanket and put it aside, then settled into Brice's chest again when they returned. Brice strummed skin with tender fingers, just touching. Jake hadn't buttoned his top shirt closed again, either.

They watched the last of the second movie and left with everyone else, not in a hurry to end their night.

"Let me grab my overnight bag from the trunk," Brice said when they reached Jake's.

Joining him at the front door, they entered the house, finding Rebecca on the couch watching TV.

"Hi Dad, Brice. Good night?" She clicked off the power on the TV and stood. She was already changed into a pajama set and her face was makeup free. Either she'd been home a while already or she was the fastest quick-change artist Brice had ever known.

"Dinner and a movie," Jake replied.

Brice was surprised he said that with an absolutely straight face. He wasn't sure he would have been able to do the same.

"Cool. We went to the theater at the mall."

"Good movie?" Jake asked.

"Yeah."

Jake locked the door and turned off all but one outside light. "Okay, bed," he told her.

She stopped on a heel and spun to say, "Oh, I forgot. I got a ninety-six on my agribusiness paper. The teacher said it was the best she'd seen on the topic."

Brice smiled, happy for her. "That's great."

"Yeah, but if mine was the only one she'd seen..." She rolled a shoulder. "Oh, well. It's going to give me a high A for the class so I'm not complaining. Stanford here I come." She bobbed her eyebrows and Brice heard Jake's low chuckle at his side. "See you in the morning."

"Night honey," Jake called as she vanished.

The house fell oddly quiet. Brice gripped the strap on his bag at his shoulder, hesitant. He wasn't sure what to do with himself, but with a subtle twist, his gaze landed on Jake and everything else faded away. "She seems very unfazed about me being here."

Jake turned out the living room light, then led Brice to the bedroom. "We took her by surprise last weekend, but I think she's okay with it." He faced Brice. "I guess this weekend really is a test with you staying over, because I can promise this. You aren't sleeping in the guest room."

Heat rose in Jake's eyes when they paused in the bedroom, a restrained need, waiting for the chance to come out and play again.

"You're amazing," Brice breathed. He lowered his bag to the corner of the bed then leaned close enough for a gentle kiss.

"I'm still kind of wound up. Would you like a glass of wine?" Jake tipped his head toward the hallway, smiling like a mischievous devil. "That's code for we need to let her get to sleep before we get nekid."

Brice agreed. "Sure, wine sounds nice."

Once they were in the kitchen, Jake drew a chilled bottle of wine from the fridge and poured a little into glasses. Holding one out for Brice, he enticed him closer with it before letting it go. "Can't wait to get you back into bed," he purred as Brice took the glass. "I completely plan on repaying the favor for tonight."

"Oh?" Brice sipped and portrayed innocent ignorance. "What favor?"

Jake closed the gap between them, standing all but chest to chest and thigh to thigh. Brice gasped when Jake's free hand cupped him through his pants. "Been dreaming all week about you, us. Want you."

Brice felt his body going limp... Well, all but one part, anyway. *That* had only faded to semi-hard and was now swiftly returning to raging beneath Jake's encouraging. Jake was leaning close to Brice's lips.

He set the wine down, anticipating that kiss.

And the phone rang.

"What the—"

Jake jumped and ran for the living room. "Hello?" he gasped, silencing the harsh shrill before it went for a second round. "What the fuck, Sissy? It's after one in the morning!" he snapped. Jake covered his face with his hand. "So take a damned cab. Why am I not surprised? Fine. Where are you? Yes, I'll come, but damn it, you better be outside. If you're not there when I pull up, you're spending the night there or in jail, do I make myself clear?" There seemed to be some kind of drama going on as Jake huffed and snarled. "I don't fucking care." He dropped his free hand to his side. "Walk outside now."

Then he hung up.

He turned and seemed to realize Brice was standing there. His expression was sorrow-filled. "Shit. I am so sorry."

"It's okay," Brice said, digging for understanding. Obviously she needed help if she couldn't get herself home.

"No, it's not. She's drunk out of her mind. Apparently, her latest dumped her at the club and she doesn't have any cash for a cab."

"Does this happen often?" Brice asked, wondering if Sissy was more of a problematic ex than he'd first assumed.

"No, but it doesn't excuse her irresponsibility." He approached and grabbed Brice with kind palms on his upper arms. "Go shower and relax. I shouldn't be too long."

"Are you sure?"

"Where are you going to go?"

Brice tried to not sigh. "You're right. I'll be fine. Go take care of her. If she's that drunk, she's not in any state to think anyway."

Jake studied him, lifting him by the chin with a tender touch. "You said a few minutes ago, I was amazing. You are so wrong." He covered Brice's lips and kissed him, a soft and lingering promise for later.

Brice's heart flipped. Reluctantly, he let Jake step away.

Jake's hands fell to his sides. "I'm going to ream her ass out for this. The first chance I've had with you and she—"

Brice silenced him with a gentle touch of a finger. "She's a part of your life and needs you right now. I'm not going anywhere." Brice could only hope this wasn't a regular thing and that she wasn't as much of a headache as he feared.

"Promise?"

Brice wanted to crawl into the heated look in Jake's gaze. "Promise."

Chapter Fifteen

Jake cruised by the nightclub and smacked the steering wheel. No Sissy in sight. "Of course not." *Like I really expected it.* He passed the doors and wound around the block to find a parking space, which took time he didn't have to spare. Time keeping him from Brice.

He reached the club's door, and got a glare from the guy taking the cover when Jake tried to bypass him.

"Trust me, I'm not staying."

"Doesn't matter," the bouncer drawled. "You walk in, you pay."

"No fucking way," he growled. Man, Sissy had him in a fit. He never swore like this.

"Look, pay or leave." The guy crossed his arms.

"Can't she be brought out?" The damned woman knew he was coming, but of course, expecting her to think of anyone beyond herself wasn't going to happen. Which meant she wasn't outside like he'd told her to be. The entire world was her lackey service.

"Nope."

"Fine." He yanked out his wallet and slapped a ten into the guy's palm.

"Enjoy," he said with a saccharin smile.

"Whatever."

The pulse of music was obnoxiously loud. Women in towering heels, absurdly short mini-skirts and obscenely tight shorts were in the center of almost every gaggle of drooling men. And to think, he'd once been one of those brainless, thinking of sex-only morons. He scooted between bodies right inside the door, to head for the bar, hunting, and had no problem finding her, surrounded by three other guys. She was waving around a drink and flirting outrageously. He wondered if any of the hounds knew she was closer to forty than thirty, even if she was dressed like the twenty-something wannabes.

"Sissy," he barked.

She jumped and blinked, then smiled in teetering intoxication. "Jakey! You're here."

"And you're leaving." He rolled the drink out of her hand and slapped it onto the bar. He gripped her arm. "You *are* leaving right now."

"Who the hell are you?" one of the guys who'd been courting her shouted over the melee.

"Her ride home. And before you ask, she's not mine. Any one of you can have her, when she's sober. Her stud dumped her tonight, so this is her pity-me party, and you have been her captive audience."

"You— You told, Jake!" She sounded like a bleating five year-old.

He only rolled his eyes. "You have five seconds to come now, or I'm going home to bed."

"With me?" She perked up so fast, he thought she was going to jump into his arms.

He reared back and accidently stepped on someone's foot. "Sorry!" he shouted at the disgruntled woman. He whipped around and scowled at Sissy. "No, not with you."

"Who is this jerk?" one of the male crowd demanded.

"My ex-husband." She waved a hand and managed to find her drink with it, quickly clasping it like a priceless treasure. "Isn't he adorable? He came to get me so I wouldn't have to take a cab."

"What?" Jake's blood was starting to boil. "You said you didn't have money for a cab. That you'd left your money at home because Denny or Danny whoever it was this week had brought you."

A couple of the guys surrounding her began to share disgruntled and unsympathetic glances.

A little red purse rose in his sight. It dangled on the end of a tether from her wrist. That was when he realized those looks were for him. He'd been played like a fiddle.

He glared at her, then bent to talk into her ear. "Fuck you, Sissy. You ruined Rebecca's life. Don't call me again." He straightened, sneering at the bar hounds. "Maybe one of your fan club will see you get home. I'm out of here."

"What?" She choked on her drink in disbelief. If she really thought he'd stay to do her bidding she was delusional along with mistaken.

He completely ignored her and shoved his way to the front of the club, doing what he should have done so many times before. Let her take care of her own messes. He'd been the gentleman one time too many, and she'd taken advantage too many times to count.

When he reached the bouncer, Jake got a sardonic grin. "Where's your passenger?"

"Sinking fangs into the next fool," he stated succinctly. "She's not my problem. Send her ass to jail if she won't leave."

"Jake! Wait!"

He stopped at the door, then uncaring and not bothering to look behind him, he strode right through it. He half hoped it smacked her in the face, not that she'd feel it.

"Jake!"

Oh, gawd. She'd followed him outside. "Go find some other dick to lie to. I know all your games, Sissy." He kept moving.

"Why don't you just stay? You're here already."

He spun and marched up to her, making her jolt to a stiff stop. She pushed curled dark brown hair out of her face, staring at him with drunk, beguiling coyness. "Because there is absolutely nothing in there I want. You already screwed up this night for me. You won't be allowed to screw up another."

Sharp nails dug into his arm when he tried to whirl away. "What?" Then her mouth twisted with jealous anger. "You had a date!"

He threw his hands outward. "Well, fuck. Yes, I did. I *am* single. What I do is none of your business." Derision dripped from his words to slice between them.

"Rebecca said you were dating a guy!" she screeched. "You're not gay!"

"I'm not having this conversation, Sissy. Go home. You're drunk off your ass."

"It's true." Her mouth fell slack. Appalled. Shocked. Disbelieving. And she wouldn't remember a word of it. He knew how she worked once she was plastered.

"Go home, Sissy. Last time. And no, I'm not taking you. You lied to me. Why I thought anything else is my mistake. You don't know how to live without lying."

"That's... That's not true!" she wailed.

"Whatever. Don't call me again. I don't care what you do, but I promise you this." He leaned close to make sure she heard every word. "If you ever hurt Rebecca because of your immaturity, you will regret it. She's old enough now to refuse to see you. Don't think I won't support that decision."

"But she's my daughter," she whispered, apparently chastised, but she didn't fool Jake in the slightest.

"Guess what? She's mine too."

"No she's not! I swear."

"God, you're so plastered." Then because Jake wasn't a complete ass to leave her wandering around the darkened streets like a wino, he gripped her elbow and tugged her to the curb. A cab rolled up at his signal. "Take her highness home." He gave the address. "And she has cash. Don't let her play on your generosity."

"Whatever you say, man," the young driver said.

Jake shut the door and watched them until they turned the corner. Finally heaving a sigh of relief that sucked the energy clear out of his toes, he made the reverse trip to his car, then to his front door.

Exhausted, but at least able to say he'd done his duty and hadn't left her alone to the predators she so keenly deserved.

As quietly as possible, he went through the house, ensuring it was locked tight. Once in his bedroom, he carefully undressed and snuck into the bathroom for a shower, in and out in under five minutes.

With the bathroom door ajar, he spotted Brice curled up on the bed, slow breaths proving he was deep asleep. The clock cursed him. He'd been gone for well over an hour and a half. Jake grumbled and sighed. Their night had officially been blown, and not in a good way.

At least he'd get to hold him. Killing all the lights, he slipped into bed beneath the covers.

"Jake?"

"Shh. I'm home. Go back to sleep." He kissed Brice's shoulder, bringing that solid body snug into his chest to relax. The fresh scent of sleep-warmed skin wrapped around him.

Not like the perfumes Sissy used to wear. This was cleaner, a little richer. He burrowed his nose into the dip of Brice's neck, kissing him softly. Contentment he hadn't felt in years eased through him. Like this was right. Like this was what had been missing. Like this was what he'd been waiting for since his and Sissy's split. After her drunken foolishness tonight, he was able to see clearly how far she'd regressed to her partying ways. Brice was nothing like her, not only physically, but there was no similarity in personality.

Brice gave when Sissy took. Brice shared when Sissy expected her share for no work.

It hit Jake with a sudden smack of shock. He was happy with Brice.

Happy.

He couldn't believe how deep that ran.

* * * *

Jake stretched, stilling when his arm brushed against hair. On his pillow. In his bed.

Then a whoosh of air slipped free and he tipped to stare at the cute blond. It had been a long time since anyone else had been in his bed.

So why did having Brice there feel so right? The sense of perfection he'd fallen asleep to while holding him remained.

Brice was lying on his stomach, facing away, the pillow pushed forward and out of the way. The thin sleep T-shirt he wore was no match for Jake's curious hand, snaking beneath the hem to caress and rub over strong muscles and firm shoulders.

Those same shoulders flexed along with a quiet moan rising from the man. Bracing himself a few inches onto an elbow he checked the clock. It was early, that predawn haze beginning to break the horizon, but with Rebecca's late night, they should still have about an hour before she'd wake up.

That was one hour he planned on enjoying with the man in his bed.

Sidling beneath the blankets, he straddled hips and worked the T-shirt higher to expose Brice's back. Kneading thumbs wove patterns first up then down, drawing him out of sleep in patient, caring waves.

"Mmm." Brice stretched and Jake felt the flex from where he touched with his palms to where he sat across strong hamstrings. With even pushes, he rolled the shirt over shoulders then off. He ran questing fingers through Brice's short hair, gripping and tugging lightly, but more furrowing, enjoying the sensation of fine, golden silk.

Then he rubbed the divots of his spine, inching ever closer to the tops of the pajamas he'd worn. A faded cotton blue, comfortable and broken in. "No pajamas tonight," he informed him.

"None?"

"No-thing," he reiterated firmly. Hooking the waist, he drew them over pale flesh and down thighs, scooting in tandem until they were bunched up at ankles, then they too were gone.

Brice was beautifully naked on his bed.

He arched forward, roaming flat palms up the backs of legs and thighs, to patiently tempt and play with the perfect rounds in front of him. Taut and well-shaped, they moved beneath him until he glided his thumbs in the crack between and lightly tugged them apart.

He swallowed. "Want to love on you," he whispered.

Brice adjusted, widening his legs and gripping the bed. "Everything you're doing feels so good."

Jake's lungs tightened, cravings and needs surging. He'd never known this amount of want. "Can I love you? Can I be inside you?"

"Jake," Brice whined with a hint of growl. "Been waiting since last night for relief."

"Why didn't—"

"Now, Jake. Just do something." He panted, his face planted into the bed as he clawed at sheets. "Now."

Jake did. He leaned forward and nipped at soft skin. Brice clenched and moaned. He repeated the torture again, getting another encouraging reaction, then he didn't stop. He licked, he kissed, he bit, thrilling at the deeper growls he got for those. He loved the sounds Brice made.

Brice was rubbing into the bed, his hips moving, rocking, and thrusting.

Clutching muscular glutes, Jake stabbed with his tongue and he swore Brice split at the seams with a shudder.

"Jake," he pleaded.

"You're sure?"

"Need you." It was graveled and hungry.

Jake hopped off the bed to strip, then opened and reached inside his night table drawer. He held what he looked for in a fist, then turned that gaze on the man in his bed and his heart tripped. He knew exactly what he wanted and said as much. "I'm going to use a condom, but I'll tell you right now, I'd like to make them unnecessary."

Brice's frame tightened then relaxed. "I'm glad to hear it." He wiggled his hips, gaining Jake's focus again.

Kneeling behind him, he eased Brice up, ensuring he was ready with extra lube. Carefully, he aligned and pressed forward to slip within the muscle, feeling tightness and friction and heat in a way he never had in his life.

He hissed, feeling for Brice's signals to either push on, or to hold back, until he was balls deep.

"Move," Brice ordered. "So full." He groaned, reaching for the wandering pillow to bite into. Growly moans still reached Jake's hearing.

With patient motions, Jake slid into his heated channel, loving everything about it. It was wholly different from loving a woman. Pleasure enveloped him in waves as pulses massaged his length with each deliberate thrust. The way Brice bucked and undulated was poetry.

Jake panted, his hands holding steady, whether to shore him up or to keep Brice near, it didn't matter. They were touching, connected, and Jake couldn't get enough of it.

His body arched, driving closer to orgasm. Heat speared him right behind his balls and he knew he didn't have long. Reaching around Brice's hip, he homed in on his dancing shaft like they'd been doing this for years. Skin slid and slipped as he pumped, his palm slick from the lube along with the added slick of his pleasure in the drops that were almost streaming from the tip.

"Fuck, Brice," he panted. "Love this." He squeezed his hand and Brice clenched in reaction. Jake's eyes crossed and he jerked, thrusting deep.

"Again. So close," Brice whimpered with an animalistic edge.

Jake pumped on the cock he held, drawing him up and twisting at the tip, the way Brice liked it. Shudders spanned his body, rolling over him in waves.

Then Brice tossed his head back, his mouth gaped in a silent cry as he shot onto the bed, hard spurts that curled his frame and wrapped around Jake's cock like a vice. He couldn't hold out any longer. He jammed himself into Brice's welcoming body, grinding and pulsating as he filled the condom.

Then all at once, he went boneless, sagging forward onto an equally limp Brice.

The only thing Jake was sorry for was making Brice wait to feel this good. There was absolutely nothing else for him to regret about loving Brice.

Chapter Sixteen

"So are you excited?" Brice carried one of the food containers to Ian's station on the lineup then placed it where he pointed.

"Ask me when I'm not sleepwalking," Ian returned. He looked up and down the line of competitors, moving shadows in the pools of light cast from streetlamps. The sun wasn't even up yet. "Cannot believe you guys talked me into this."

"If you hate it, don't do it again, but I think you have a shot at winning." Caleb stopped setting up the table, laying it on its side and walked to his husband to give him a slow kiss. Brice tried to look away, but still, they were hot to watch. "Now finish setting up. You have to get the brisket ready to go on by time at five."

"That's another thing," Ian grumbled. "Three-thirty in the morning. You do know I'm not twenty any longer, right?"

"Quit yer bitchin'," Caleb replied, as unconcerned as Brice had ever heard. "You can sleep later, all day tomorrow."

Brice just shook his head, hiding his laughter. Watching these guys go back and forth was like a comedy skit. Ian only did it because he knew Caleb wouldn't take it and generally poked right back. They played so well off each other, it really was like watching an old married couple, even though they'd only been together a few years.

"The others are coming today to help out, too, right?" Brice asked.

"Yep. Jessie should be here in a couple of hours with Bethany and the boys. Wanda will be by with drinks. With Jake at your place, that's everybody."

"So see, Ian? A full army for you." Brice helped tie down the leg of the shade canopy, which would sit between the grill line and the truck tailgate. There had to be a certain distance between the grills and the vehicles for safety. It was really too early for Brice for that much technical thinking. Just tell him what to do, what to hold, and where to stand, and he was good to go.

"Jake is coming, isn't he?" Caleb asked a few minutes later.

"He'll be here with Rebecca, probably about nine or so. I told him to go ahead and sleep a little more, which looked like it was a good suggestion. We'd be tripping over each other out here this morning."

"He hasn't driven you nuts yet, huh?" Ian joked, giving Caleb a broad smile that was full of faked innocence.

"Not yet."

Sissy on the other hand... Ever since that night she'd called Jake for drunken help, she'd been a thorn in both their sides. Bothering Jake about the littlest things, which in turn stole Jake's time and attention from Brice. If Brice didn't know any better, he'd swear Sissy was as jealous as any woman could be. Now that she'd seen Jake happy, and it wasn't with her, she'd realized he wasn't playing games in moving on without her. He wiped a hand over his brow and propped his ass against the slack tailgate. He didn't want to think about her. She wasn't anywhere near

Jasper and that put her even further from himself and Jake.

"We haven't seen each other much since school let out. He's had some late nights and Rebecca is taking a summer Driver's Ed course."

"She'll be hearing from Stanford soon, won't she?" Caleb popped the lid on a steaming cup of coffee and took a sip. He murmured his appreciation. "Love your coffee, Ian. Have I told you that?"

"Not in the last twenty minutes," he deadpanned.

"Smartass."

"Yep."

Brice shook his head, grinning lightly. *Oh, right Stanford.* "Probably in the next week or so. She took the tour last fall and has been one of the most driven kids I've seen in a long time."

Caleb nodded. "She's a smart cookie."

"The whole lot of them are a great bunch. I wish I had more like them in my classes."

"Nah, then you'd get spoiled." Caleb sipped some more coffee then passed it over to Ian.

"Spoil me! Please!" Brice cried, laughing. After the whole knifing incident, he was ready for a string of good kids.

Ian braced the tall cup and took a healthy sip, sighing afterward. They were so happy together. They literally could finish each other sentences if they tried. Brice wondered if that was where he and Jake were heading. Or if this was really just a summer fling between them. He wished he knew.

He cared a lot for Jake, and Rebecca meant the world to him. They all talked a lot when they were together, and she'd taken a genuine interest in his garden when she was at his place. Always asking questions. Never shy about wanting to lend a hand.

Unlike many of the modern kids that talked nonstop about whatever video game was out, or what reality TV show was a must-watch, she loved his garden.

Unfortunately, having a common interest in gardening didn't really cement any type of relationship. The sex was unbelievable with Jake. They'd just never talked about the step that would take what they shared further, or if it was even intentioned for them to go that far. If this was only sex, he was fine with that, if he knew the score. Unfortunately, he didn't know for sure, and he knew his heart was too deeply entrenched now to pretend he wasn't involved.

That crush he'd had for the youngest Drew brother had grown into something he was afraid to put into words.

"Okay, time to get the grill set to spark." Ian dusted off his hands. "Almost done with this leg of it."

"Lead on, McDuff." Brice waved a hand and was put to work again.

* * * *

The sun had fully risen and was well on its way to reaching July Fourth temperatures before the end of the day.

Crowds walked past the barbecue pits, some stopping to chat with friends and familiar faces, others wanting to get a non-competition snack or see what was on the menu for the lunchtime crowd.

Ian seemed genuinely surprised when several people stopped to talk to him specifically. Yes, this was his first year. No, he didn't know if he'd be doing it again. No, he wasn't worried about the competition. He was there to see how he stacked up.

Winning would be a by-product. Brice lost count of the number of times Ian had that conversation, verbatim.

People started showing up to lend a hand also. Bethany with food. Wanda with drinks to sell and for them.

Jeannie was on bed rest for the next two weeks as her due date approached. Brice smiled and shook hands, talked to students, their parents, and people he knew. It felt good. He was comfortable. And he had his pseudo-family, Ian and Caleb, and by extension, all of Caleb's family.

He was home.

A hard slap on his shoulder jerked him out of his thoughts and aimless mental wandering. He whirled and gaped at the man behind him. He had to be imagining this. "Tucker?"

"Little Bri-Bri!"

"Holy shit! Tucker," he choked out, swallowed by muscled arms and almost swung around off his feet. "Put me down! How'd you find me? What are you doing here?" Then, "Are you by yourself?" he added with much cooler meaning.

"Yeah, I'm alone. Mom doesn't know I'm here."

"Not surprised," he scoffed. "Let me introduce you before the cop arrests you for manhandling the locals."

"Cop?" Tucker's eyes bulged, and he took a step away. "Uh, I'm clean, Bri."

"Shut up. I know. He's family. Just don't be an ass." He led his older brother to the group congregated around the sales table. "Hey!" Everyone looked up. First at him, then at the monster behind him. Okay, monster was a bit much, but really, he was Brice's brother. He could call him whatever he wanted.

"This is Tucker, my older brother. Say hi."

"Hi," came a unified grunt. Brice arched an eyebrow and Ian and Wanda both snickered.

"Sorry." She held out a hand. "I'm Wanda. Just giving him hell." She jabbed a finger at Brice's arm and he flinched to hide tender body parts.

Ian and Caleb both shook. Tucker took one look and said, "You're the cop."

Caleb swept his gaze up and down. "Wow, he's good."

"I've met a few, and not always under the best circumstances."

"Okay. That's everyone who's here."

"There's more?"

Brice laughed, really feeling the truth of it when he said, "In this family, there's a whole town. Be back in a few," he called with a wave to let them know he'd be fine, leading Tucker away. When it was doubtful they'd hear anything, he asked, "Okay, why are you here?" He leaned against the corner of the town gazebo in the opposite corner of the pit crews and crossed his arms. Waiting. With each dragged out minute, his stomach twisted around a little more. Tucker showing up unannounced was not a good sign. Not when they'd made it all so clear they wanted nothing to do with their youngest boy. Not when the entire family had turned their back on him after he'd told them the truth and quit hiding. At least he'd already been out of the house and no longer relying on them for his future, his meals, or his wellbeing.

"Because I wanted to see you."

"Bullshit. I moved away from home and it wasn't fast enough to see the back of my head for Dad."

"Bri, I'm serious. I wanted to see you."

His teeth ground at his brother's evasion. People milled around unseen, kids running wildly, parents smiling and friends laughing and talking. None of it filtered in behind the irritation and hidden anger. "Not telling me why. And how did you find me? I thought they had, and I quote, 'made me dead' to the family."

Tucker's expression paled, sorrow making him more sallow than even his usual Irish white skin, like Brice's, allowed for. "Dad's dead. He died last winter."

That hit Brice with an unexpected impact, chilling him when he shouldn't have felt anything but sunshine and heat. He gasped like he'd been sucker punched, bending over, a hand finding his knee to brace himself from pitching forward. Sounds and voices swirled into a vortex. He heaved for air. His lungs clenched, fighting him for every molecule, every atom of oxygen. Every draw tasted arid and bitter. He didn't know how long he waited for it to pass.

"When?" he croaked.

"He had a heart attack in February. I started looking for you in earnest then. Mom refused to give me any information. Do you have any idea how many Brice Reynolds there are in this country?" He edged closer, a helping hand under an arm to bring him horizontal again. "It took this long to find you, and I'm sorry that it did."

"Hey! Let go of him!"

Brice watched Rebecca tackle a much taller Tucker, clinging to him, pummeling him with fists while he tried to fight off a five-foot four inch dynamo of a protector.

"Stop!" Brice shouted. He covered his face and sank to the ground, unable to hold his own weight.

"What did you do to him?" she demanded. Brice didn't hear anything else as his heart pounded between his ears and he swallowed sobs.

Chapter Seventeen

Jake didn't know what to think. One minute he and Rebecca were walking across the commons for the cook-off lineup then she's tackling some giant blond guy who seemed to be doing something to Brice. Maybe.

Then Brice collapsed to the ground and everything else ceased to matter.

"Brice!" People were gawking as he sprinted to the man on the ground. "Baby, are you hurt?"

Jake fell onto his knees on the grass and pulled Brice into his chest. His head shook hard, his body trembling within Jake's wrapped arms.

"What happened? Rebecca you can let him go," he said.

Grudgingly, and very distrusting, she let the tall guy go, though she didn't move too far away. He didn't seem intent on escaping, or doing much of anything.

"Nothing to see here," she snapped, shooing away onlookers. "What did you do to Brice?" She glared daggers at the guy she'd tackled that would frighten a knife-throwing junkie.

"Nothing!" He held out his hands. "I'm his brother."

"What are you doing here? Last I heard, he had no family." Jake didn't hide the deep scorn in his voice. He knew perfectly well why he had no family.

"Brice, tell them, please."

Brice shook like a leaf, panting and gasping in stuttered waves. Moist heat hit Jake's throat. Jake petted his neck and shoulder, waiting for him calm down enough to explain something, anything.

"Come on, baby. Tell me you're okay," Jake whispered, rocking him gently, ignoring everything and everyone else in the world for the man in his arms.

"Up." A single gasp of breath.

It was all Jake heard and he obeyed without question. Brice clung, an arm wrapped around Jake's waist like he was attached there.

"Do you need anything? Are you hurt?" Brice didn't look like he'd been injured again, with his wound from the school year healed. Except he was being so slow to answer, to show any reaction except shock, Jake didn't know what to think.

Sluggishly, he straightened. It took as long, if not longer for him to breathe normally. Jake kept an eye on him until he began to see color returning to his blanched face. He caressed the side of Brice's jaw, ignoring the stupefied and unsure looks of the moron standing over them.

"Better." He flexed fingers, digging into Jake's side as he found strength to stand again on his own two feet. He rested his forehead to Jake's shoulder, each draw of breath seeming to come easier to him. "Didn't mean to scare you," he whispered for Jake.

"Just so long as you're okay." He stroked a thumb over a cheek. "You are okay, right?"

Brice nodded, a smile ghosting over his lips. "Yeah, just..."

He straightened to gaze into Jake's eyes, and in that instant he knew the truth. Jake would die without the man in his arms. Green eyes sparkled within a face that was dearer to him than any other person's alive, with the one exception of his daughter. They'd spent two weekends together since that first trip Brice took to Des Moines to stay with Jake, and after all the weeks, all the time, Jake accepted what he felt wasn't a mirage. It was real. Very, very real.

"This is my brother, Tucker. Tucker, Jake Drew. The youngest brother to the cop you met earlier."

"Uh, hello," Tucker greeted, unsure. "Are you...with... Um." Tucker kept bouncing between Jake and Brice, then ran a hand over his mouth, probably swallowing things that wouldn't go over well at the moment, or ever. Neither offered a hand to shake. He wasn't about to let Brice go to do it anyway.

"Yes," Brice stated with conviction. "So if you don't like it, leave now."

Jake was startled to hear the underlying growl in Brice's voice. He wasn't the aggressive type, at all. Tucker stayed where he was, though his expression didn't really clear. Like he was trying to adjust to seeing his brother with a man.

Jake didn't give two shits what Tucker thought.

"How did you find me?" Brice asked.

"The usual ways. Phone listings, school pages. I didn't think you'd give up teaching, and I was right."

Rebecca inched up and stood by Jake's shoulder, eyeing Tucker warily. "I'm going to go find Terra. If he does anything to Brice, kick his ass."

Jake arched an eyebrow and Brice snorted. With a kiss on Jake's cheek, she left, but not before giving one last warning glare to the other blond.

"So are you staying or leaving?" Brice demanded.

"At least for today, staying."

"Fine." Brice released Jake but threaded fingers together. "I need a drink. Just wish it came on the rocks."

Jake didn't know what had happened, but he wasn't going to leave Brice's side. When they approached the cooking lineup, Jake noticed several people were gathered in a huddle.

"What happened?" Brice asked as they neared.

Jake's first thought was what else was going to happen or go wrong. It wasn't even ten in the morning.

Caleb broke away from the group, his keys in his hand. "Jeannie went into labor a few minutes ago. I'm taking Wanda to go with her to the hospital."

Wanda was jittery, flitting back and forth and wide-eyed, her purse in one hand, her keys in another as she bounced around, nearly out of control with anxiety. Brice slid free of Jake's hold and gripped Wanda's arms, jolting her to a stiff stop. "Look at me," he directed in a low order. He held her immobile until she did. "It's going to be okay. Jeannie is strong as an ox and too much of a bitch to let anything go wrong."

Wanda barked a sharp, anxious laugh.

"You've taken the classes. She needs you right now to keep her sane. That means you have to be calm. Deep breath." He waited while she did. "You're going to be great mothers. You've been waiting for this day. It's Christmas in July."

"I know," she croaked then cleared her throat. "I'm okay." She wiped her eyes. "Ready or not, huh?"

"Ready or not," he agreed. He kissed her gently on the cheek. "Let Caleb drive and get you there."

"We'll call with updates." She smiled at the group. "Thank you, all of you." Then she jogged around to catch up with Caleb's longer strides.

"How many of you are there?" Tucker said with distracted confusion.

"How many what?" Brice bristled. Tension radiated off his shoulders.

"Uh... Never mind."

"Probably the smartest two words of your life," Jake muttered.

The group grew quiet, helping Ian as they needed. The kids popped in occasionally to see what was going on. But everyone was waiting for word from Wanda or Caleb.

Chaos of the day was in full swing as people coming for the day's events filled the commons and street block, perusing the cooking teams and crafts vendors on the other side of the set-up. Tucker was introduced yet again. He seemed taken by surprise at the group of friends that surrounded not only Brice, but by the community who quickly came to learn about Jeannie's pending birth.

"I have sides in containers already to give out on the plates once Ian has turned in his judging boxes."

"Great," Brice said, helping Bethany get organized. He smiled right at Jake, encouraging Jake to relax further. Whatever had happened between Brice and his brother would have to wait until later, but at least Brice appeared to be calm for now.

Noon rolled up on them and the first boxes were turned in. Jake marked everything and carried it to the judges' table. It was a blind judging so he signed off on the box and the organizers did the rest.

The scent of wood smoke, charcoal, barbecue sauce and all kinds of spices and meat permeated the air in the hot July sunlight. Morning rolled into afternoon, and as the hours ticked past, the crew mechanics smoothed out, taking turns to give everyone breaks to check out the rest of the party on the commons. A live band had started to play just after lunchtime and people were bunched around to listen.

An entire side of the block had games and two inflated bouncy houses for the kids. Mayhem and chaos seemed to be the soundtrack for the day.

A cell phone chirped and like a machine, every person on Ian's crew froze. He pulled out his phone, then nodded when he saw the screen. "Yeah?" Slowly, he began to beam, a smile splitting his face. "Woohoooo! Six pounds ten ounces. Ten toes. Ten fingers. Got it." He winked as everyone else laughed or chuckled. "That is wonderful. Is Wanda still standing?" He laughed uproariously, motioning that he'd tell when he was done talking. "Okay. See you in a bit. Love to the girls."

Ian disconnected. "Wanda almost got thrown out of the delivery room. She tried to take the doctor's place because he wasn't treating Jeannie right. Your guess is as good as mine as to what *right* is in that woman's mind, but they're all fine. Jeannie will be in a room shortly and home by Monday. Caleb said they both did well, and the baby is a peach."

A cheer went up from all of them, which turned heads and brought news-seekers.

"One heck of a July Fourth celebration," a guy said approaching the table. Ian reached out and shook his hand.

"Hey, Lonnie. Yep. Jeannie just hatched. An Independence Day baby."

"That's great news."

Jake listened with half an ear as gossip flew like birds off a tree branch. He noticed Brice and Tucker had slipped to the edge of the setup and were talking again. All he knew was he better not cause Brice any more pain. He'd suffered enough from a family who refused to understand and had rejected him because of it.

* * * *

Brice leaned backward against the truck side wall, crossing his arms to study his brother. Now that the first rush was off the grill, things were a lot less tense and Ian was relaxing. Plus with Caleb and Wanda gone, it was actually easier to move around. He was thrilled to hear the girls were okay and their daughter had made a safe arrival. He knew those two women had been more than a little strung out waiting. It wasn't any surprise to him that Wanda had lost all sense of direction and thought when Jeannie went into labor. They'd been together since high school, and best friends before that.

Tucker stood beside him, though little else had been said really since their first conversation. He had a couple of inches on Brice and his hair was a few shades darker, but it was also redder. Other than that, there wasn't much else different between the brothers. He'd hardly changed in the years since Brice had left West Virginia and he'd never looked back.

"So you really came all this way to tell me about Dad?"

"In part, yeah." Tucker sighed and took up the same position beside Brice. "Would you think about coming home?"

"I am home," Brice pointed out. "I was a shadow in our house until I moved out because I wanted to be a teacher, then I became history when I told everyone I was gay. I stayed long enough to get my certificate and nothing improved. There's nothing for me there." Watching his brother out of the corner of his eye, he said, "Does Mom even know you're here?" *Betting she doesn't.* And he was proven right with Tucker's reply.

"No. I don't answer to her any more than you did once you moved out."

"Yet, I've been gone since I was twenty. So, I've been dead for, what? Thirteen years now? And *now* you want to be brothers?"

"We've always been brothers, Brice."

"Maybe. But you stopped being family when you turned your back on me and didn't try to change it until the person who could make you pay for going against the law of the land is dead."

"You've changed," Tucker said, gaping at Brice.

"I have. I've learned who I can rely on, and who I can't." He glanced over his shoulder at the people he'd come to call friends in the last three years. Facing forward, he said, "I can't change being gay, any more than you can change being straight. My family accepts that."

"How many of them are gay?"

"Why?"

Tucker cleared his throat, seeking in the direction Brice just had then returning to his previous near-sulking position. "I've never seen so many people so happy."

"It's been hard earned in this town. Not everyone likes us being here, but we have as much right as you do, or the next person." He absently put a palm over the reminder of exactly those who didn't believe Brice and people like him should even be allowed to breathe. *At least for the most part, they're coming around,* "So you're really that happy here?"

Brice didn't even have to think about that. "Yes. I am. I have a wonderful and supportive family of friends. A boyfriend who I care more for than just about anything on this great big rock of a planet, and a career that I love in a district that respects me." He sighed. "I might get half of that back in West Virginia, but why should I settle?"

Tucker didn't answer right away, and Brice feared he was looking for other arguments.

"This looks like every other small town I've ever seen, but it sounds, and even feels…"

"Like home," Brice suggested.

"Yeah." Tucker sighed. He lowered his chin to his chest. "Do you still want to be brothers?"

"Never said I didn't. What I am saying is that I'm not going to be something I'm not to keep anyone else happy anymore." Brice stood straight and put a hand on Tucker's arm. "Think about it, because if the family did it to me, you'll be considered a traitor and they'll likely do the same to you. Make sure any challenges in the face of their values and beliefs are worth being disowned over before you go that far."

"How'd you do it?" Tucker asked seriously.

"I didn't have a choice." Brice smiled sadly. "I have to get back to help Ian win this cook-off. You're welcome to stay and help."

"I need to think for a while. I won't leave without saying goodbye."

"Whatever you decide." Brice let him go and walked away.

Chapter Eighteen

Jake wiped his hands on a moist towel, tossing it in the closest lined bucket when he was done. "I never knew I could eat that much brisket." He patted his overly full stomach and leaned back in the folding camping chair. "Damn, Ian. I swear it's getting better."

Ian shot him a huge grin. "Still think I have a chance?"

"I'd be shocked if you didn't," Jake retorted, convinced. "I'm sold."

A cold soda appeared at his shoulder. "Thanks, baby." He smiled and Brice returned it. He hadn't pushed, though Brice had been quiet and withdrawn since the conversation he'd had with his brother. He'd noticed at some point, Tucker had vanished. What that meant, he didn't know.

"It's almost four. Aren't they about to call this thing?" Jessie yawned from another chair, a foot hooked over his knee. He looked like a nap was calling him hard.

"Any time now," Ian informed him. The food was mostly gone, a few people still coming by sporadically to buy plates. "Really appreciate everyone's help."

"You're welcome." Jake saluted with his soda can. "I think just about everyone is ready to pass out."

"You?" Brice snickered from behind his shoulder. "I was up before the roosters to help set up."

Jake reached out, hunting for a hand and tugged when he found it. Brice teetered then sank down to his lap. "Everything okay?" He sifted fingers into Brice's hair.

"Mostly. With Tucker, I don't know."

"What happened earlier?"

"I'll tell you when we get home," Brice answered with an evasive reply. He burrowed into Jake's shoulder and relaxed, looping arms around him to hold on tight. Jake repaid the favor, not pushing for what Brice wasn't willing to share, snuggling him into his body with an arm because that really was the most important thing for him.

Home. It sounded wonderful. To never have to spend a night, much less a whole week or more, apart. But...whose house? Brice's life was there, in Jasper. His job. And without a doubt, his friends.

Jake had his house, a few friends, and Jessie. His job.

But there's no Sissy in Jasper.

The insidiously gleeful voice almost made him cheer with realization. He'd be completely free of her. Rebecca was going to college in the fall. That meant he didn't necessarily have to keep the house, either.

All that really left was his job. He could commute once a week and work from home. He had the tools and the programs he needed, he'd simply never bothered. The agency he worked for had several contract accounts that Jake only saw once a quarter, so it wasn't impossible.

That only left one question. The answer needed from one man. Were they ready to take it to the next step? Was he? They'd only been together a few months. Jake replayed snippets since he'd become friends with the man currently curled up like a puppy on his lap.

Had he noticed any other men? He sipped at his can carefully to not disturb a dozing Brice. He couldn't recall one man who had drawn anything near to interest. What about women? He'd looked, but again, the answer was no. Not even the night he'd gone to pull Sissy out of the nightclub had he given more than a sneering glance at all the skin, push-up tits, and flaunted sexuality. It surprised him with a whip of awareness that he *hadn't* looked, hadn't found any of them even the least bit desirable, or attractive. There'd been blondes, brunettes, short, tall, stacked and modest. It hadn't mattered. None of them had appealed to him in the least.

Did that mean he was fully gay? Could he commit himself to Brice, man to man?

He lazily watched people strolling and chatting, laughing between couples and parents, friends and who knew who else. Some of the women were pretty. Shirts or summer dresses that could be modest, or sweetly seductive. He let his eyes travel at chest height and lingered in appreciation only to flicker on as someone else filled his focus. Meaning no one grabbed his attention for long, or kept it as an individual. On the other hand, several passing men were packing with all the right angles, like a tower, solidly built. But... They weren't pulling at him either.

Neither men nor women wholly held his attention for more than a span of seconds as he studied them and his reactions to them.

Maybe it wasn't that they didn't matter but because he was already holding the one person, even if he was male, that carried all of Jake's affection in the palm of one hand.

Maybe not one person drew his interest or was considered attractive because he really didn't need anyone else.

But did that make him gay?

He rested his chin on the top of Brice's head. He didn't think it did.

What it did tell him was he was in love with the only person who could hold his attention, and thus his affection. Was there really a need to label it? He was in love. What else needed to be defined?

Nothing.

Finishing his drink, he dropped the can with a toss into the refuse bucket and wound his hands over Brice's weight to hold him steady while he rested. Jake knew he'd been going almost nonstop all day, not only as backup for Ian but helping with sales and clean up, especially once Caleb had left with Wanda. He wasn't sure when Caleb would be coming back so he knew Brice would be staying to bring it all down again. Ian had started cooling off the grill some time ago. He didn't think it would be too much later to finally be able to walk through someone's front door and claim a chair or a couch for a few hours.

"Hey! They're calling everyone up!" someone shouted as he jogged past the tables, spreading the message.

"All right!" Ian clapped his hands once and straightened.

Jessie stayed in his chair, content to not move and watch things while they took in the celebrations.

"You guys coming?" Ian gave a kind look to an exhausted Brice.

Jake nudged the sleeping lump on his lap. "Wake up, cute stuff."

Brice mumbled then pulled away from Jake's chest and blinked. He wobbled unsteadily when he found his legs, but Jake caught him. Holding his hand, they all walked up to the gazebo to hear the sponsor's announcements and the mayor's spiels to hand out prizes.

One by one, ribbons were awarded along with gift cards. There was jovial laughter of congratulations and back slapping as teams cheerfully took their winnings.

"Now, it is my pleasure to announce the overall first and second place winners. This year, I'm pleased to say we had three first-time teams, two of which are from right here in town." Cheering rolled through the crowd. Ian raised a hand and waved when he was named, getting some congenial ribbing from friends and competitors alike. "Also, thanks to the contributions and donations from Jasper's own town businesses, we were able to pull together a couple of nice prizes. Let me tell you, this was a mighty difficult decision." He rubbed his rather soft stomach and laughed, winking at the crowd. "I wasn't judging, but I hold no shame is saying I ate, and I ate plenty!"

Another round of laughter added a layer to the building anticipation.

"So let me get to it, right?" He shook the page in his hand in exclamation. "The runner-up for champion for this year's July Fourth All Area Cook-off is..." He swept the crowd with a wide look and held breath, drawing them in. "Is... Mr. Lockney and Sons!"

A spry older man and two older boys trooped up to the gazebo steps to shake hands and hear congratulations. They hammed it for a few seconds getting their picture taken for the paper.

Standing next to Ian, Jake felt his tension dissipate. He hadn't been called yet and had less faith than his friends did apparently. Not necessarily superstitious, but willing to add a little extra hope, Jake crossed his finger and waited.

"This year's champion is one of those first-timers, and let me tell you, we all were taken by surprise by what this man turned in. Why, you may ask? Well, I expect him to know a truck grill from the inside out, but not a barbecue grill. Ian Cravelle! Get up here!"

"Holy shit," he breathed, standing stock-still frozen and stunned, with slow-dawning realization.

Jake nudged him, grinning at him without shame. "That's you, bro."

"No shit." He leaped into the air with a fist pump. "Hot damn!"

Several laughed and made way for him as he trotted up to the front of the crowd. "For our champion, we have this lovely trophy." A pretty girl in a western shirt handed it to him. He got a kiss on the cheek at the same time.

"Honey, he's married!" an unknown female voice cried from the audience.

More laughter erupted.

"And we also have this nice little check for five hundred dollars!" The roar of applause and cheers became deafening. The announcer said a few more words, which for the most part, Jake completely missed. Brice leaned into his shoulder. A happy sigh and winsome smile radiated his pleasure in seeing his friends win.

"You did good today." He kissed Brice's head, squeezing his hand. "You know he would have totally backed out if he'd been left alone."

"Uh huh," came the sublime sigh. "I am so wiped."

"A hot shower and a back rub sound like a good idea?"

Brice tipped his head to gaze at him from behind lowered lashes. "Sounds like a great idea."

* * * *

By Sunday, Brice was positive Tucker had left town even though he'd given his brother his address. He hadn't seen him since their conversation the day before and didn't know where he was staying. Saturday night, after a long day helping Ian, Brice had received the royal treatment from Jake. A hot shower, a cooked dinner, and that back rub, which had culminated in a sensual round of blowjobs. He hadn't meant to, but he was positive he passed out right after that. It had been one of the longest Saturdays in a long time, with Ian, then Wanda and Jeannie's delivery. She hadn't returned, not that Brice had expected her to. Caleb had reappeared a little after four to hear all about Ian's win and share in the moment. Cleaning up had taken far less time than when they'd set-up that morning since they had almost no food to worry about.

Now Sunday, he was planning on taking it slow and easy. A little TLC for his garden and just doing nothing with a book or watching TV for a few hours. Hopefully curled up with Jake in some manner.

Except his plans were derailed by Jake saying, "I should probably head home a little early today. There's a few things I need to look into and I want to get started on them."

Brice finished putting the last of the dishes away from that morning. "Oh." He didn't turn around from the cabinet in front of him. The disappointment he felt would be all over his face. He didn't want to cage Jake, but hearing how excited Jake was to go home, chilled him.

He was attempting to calm his racing heart when strong arms encircled his waist and a light kiss hit his shoulder. "Hey," Jake whispered. "What happened? I don't think I've heard you give that lackluster of an answer, to anything."

I don't want you to go. "Nothing." When he was confident enough he'd managed to erase his apprehension from his features, he slowly turned in the arms that held him. "You're right. It's a long drive."

"Brice." Jake shook his head, chiding him gently. "Whatever you're thinking, you're wrong."

"Are you coming back?" he managed, not wanting to let on how much Jake's words had hurt. He wasn't ready to let him leave, to not see him for another week, or longer. They'd had so little time together that weekend, he'd been counting on Sunday.

"Am I?" Jake reared back a smidge, surprise in his wide eyes.

"Never mind." Brice was pushing too hard. He had to remember this was still new for Jake, that he hadn't been into guys for decades, or been in a relationship for nearly half as long.

Jake was pulling away, literally and figuratively. Sometime over the last three days, something had changed for Jake. Brice had hoped it had been imagined, but by Saturday night, there was a secret in Jake's blue eyes, and Brice didn't know how to read it. Maybe all the attention the night before had a different meaning, a particular purpose.

It looked like Brice was going to be the loser in this relationship after all. He hadn't meant to care this much, to let that old crush turn into something this profound when he knew the odds. He more than cared for the man holding him.

He loved Jake Drew. Down deep where it counted. "Baby, don't—"

A knock interrupted Jake.

"I got it!" Rebecca called from the living room.

Brice didn't try to stop her.

Just a few months ago, no one in town aside from Caleb and Ian knew either Rebecca or Jake, and now they were a common fixture, and part of Brice's world. He blinked when the hurt grew. He was going to miss them both. He hadn't realized how he'd started to feel like they were a family, together, when Jake and Rebecca came to stay with him.

"Brice, look at me." A firm hand under his jaw made sure he did. "I'll be back."

Brice guessed at how that was meant. A fling. "I want you to come back." He lifted a shoulder, trying for light-hearted when he felt anything but. "And I know you have to go home." He was sure his smile looked as limp as it felt. He'd just hoped he wouldn't have to say goodbye for another six hours, and be better prepared for it.

The sound of shuffled feet drew Brice's attention over Jake's shoulder. A slightly embarrassed Tucker stood in the kitchen entryway.

"Sorry, didn't mean to interrupt."

Chapter Nineteen

"You didn't," Jake said. He gave Brice a tender look followed by an even gentler kiss then let him go. "I guess you two have a lot to talk about."

Not as important as you! Brice just managed to catch that, aiming over Jake's shoulder instead, "Make yourself at home, Tucker. Let me tell them goodbye."

"Sure, sure," he said in a rush.

He stepped out of sight and Brice focused on Jake again.

"Why do I get the feeling you're looking at this all wrong?" Jake said.

"Looking at what? I know you have to go home. I just don't like it, okay?" Brice bit his lip, wishing that hadn't slipped out, wishing he hadn't let his own feelings come that close to the surface.

A slow smile curved Jake's lips. "More than okay. Because I don't want to go either. Not ever," he breathed.

Brice blinked then tipped his head. "What are you saying?"

"Let me get a few things at least in the works, and we'll sit down and talk." He palmed Brice's jaw between both hands and held him perfectly still. "I don't want to jump into anything blindly. Did that once already. One thing I do know is you're not a mistake, of any kind."

Brice swallowed. He nodded, silently, suddenly, hoping. Was he jumping to conclusions? To have his emotions swinging so precariously? Probably. He'd never realized how terrifying it was to love like this. He was even more terrified of getting his hopes up only to have them wrecked.

He evened out his voice with effort. "So, you are coming back?

"Let me put it this way," Jake purred with sexual lust. He lowered to Brice's lips and kissed him. Not just a feathery kiss like the one a moment ago, but a devouring kiss, one that rocked Brice on his heels and had him clutching at clothing to stay upright. His knees quaked in a way he'd only read about. And it wasn't supposed to happen to guys. Jake tunneled fingers into Brice's hair to lock him into place as he tipped Brice's world.

They were both panting when Jake finally let him go.

"Just a few things," he reiterated. "I'll call tonight to let you know we're home."

"You better." Brice poked his chest with a finger.

"I will. I promise," he said, smiling. "Suddenly I wish Tucker wasn't sitting out there. Want to get you naked so badly."

"Am I awful to say I agree with you?" Brice finally relinquished the firm grip he had on his control and sank into Jake's embrace, holding him, savoring. It was going to be a long break until he saw his man again. Now he understood why long distance relationships sucked, and why they rarely made it. It was torture to not be together.

* * * *

Brice sat on the couch next to his brother after he'd said a final goodbye to Jake and Rebecca. "So, what did you decide?"

"Honestly?"

Brice rolled his eyes. "No, lie to me. I have all the time in the world." He scooted into the corner and crossed his arms.

"I'd forgotten what a brat you could be." Though Tucker was smiling as he said it.

"I haven't forgotten what an ass you could be," Brice warned him with a meaningful scowl.

Tucker had the nerve to at least look guilty. "Yeah, I know. And I'm sorry. I should have said that earlier."

"So if Mom doesn't know you're here, and you're the reason I know about Dad, they really had no intention of ever letting me know, did they?"

Tucker fell silent. His head hung low. "I won't speak for Mom, but I knew you should be told. Regardless, you are still and will always be my brother." He drew a breath. "I know you'd have no way to know, but I was married for about four years. Her name was Doreen. We divorced about two years ago." Like he was offering a bridge, an olive branch, to start mending the distance.

"Oh? Any kids?"

"No, thankfully. I wouldn't have wanted to put them through a divorce and after the honeymoon, well we went south fast."

"I'm sorry."

Tucker fell silent. "I've given a lot of thought since her to what I want to do and where. I know Mom can be toxic in her opinions. She's grown worse since you... Since..."

Brice fluttered a hand. "Just spit it out. I've heard it all and then some."

"Well, since you told everyone you were gay." He rolled his jaw, as though trying to find the right words. "I'm sorry for blindly following, even when I knew it was wrong. I mean, we were brothers before you became someone who slept with guys."

Brice coughed a harsh sound. "I would hope so. I doubt Mom was really ever that delicate." He pursed his lips as he said that, proving he knew exactly how their mother would have reacted. "So, what are you going to do? You know she's going to pitch a fit mountain-style when she learns you've found me and dare I say it? Spoken. And you let me live."

"I need to think on it a little more, but I think I already know."

Brice raised his hand to make him pause. "Before you make that choice, know that if you do, people in this town do not tolerate injustice, or hatred. In fact, the last guy who attempted it is in jail."

"Wow. What did he do?"

"Tried to kill me."

After Tucker remembered to breathe, he shook his head, staring at Brice like he'd grown a second head. "No shit! What happened?"

"One of my seniors wanted dear daddy's approval and came to school with a knife. That knife found me."

For only the second time since reappearing in Brice's life, Tucker reached out and unceremoniously yanked Brice into his chest. Brice grunted, bracing his hands on shoulders. "Fucking shit! And you never called home? Never said anything?"

Brice laughed, though it was caustic. "Uh, I had no family to call home to, remember?" After almost being mauled, Brice extracted himself. "I'm fine." He pulled up his shirt to prove it, baring the shrunken scar. Even the sutures were gone now. Tucker gaped soundlessly for seconds. "I had a few close minutes, but after they sewed everything up, it was all done except for healing." Lowering his shirt, he settled again. "In fact, that was how Jake and I really got close. He was the volunteer to stay with me while I was recovering the first few days."

Tucker rubbed his hands down his face. "Unbelievable. And they never would have known if you'd died." Brice was surprised to see him trembling. "I never would have known," he choked out.

"Now do you see what their prejudice and hate cost us?" Brice cupped Tucker's shoulder in support. So much more than just lost time. "They called me dead to the family. There is nothing for me in West Virginia."

Tucker swallowed thickly, sniffing and clearing his throat. Roughly, he nodded. "What's funny is now that I don't live *at* home, I see more like you, or maybe, more people who aren't hiding. I see them holding hands, with their kids at the park, or even just out. It's something Mom or Dad would never see, or agree with."

"See, that's just it," Brice told him gently. "It's not up to them to agree with anything. I don't agree with a lot of religions and their values, but I acknowledge they have that right. How I live is the same thing. Just like where I want to live, what job I want. They have no power over who I care for."

"And you really like him, don't you?"

"I do, Tucker. I'm not sure where we'll end up, but I have hopes."

He nodded, steadying his breathing. "Then I think my mind is made up." He relaxed finally to the back of the couch, half facing Brice. "I didn't tell you at first, but I also came out here because I'm looking for work. I nosed around a little when it looked like I'd finally found you, and I think I have some good leads." For the first time, Tucker seemed unsure. "That is, if you can forgive me and still want a brother?"

"No more bullshit? What they did was cruel, just for starters."

"I know. No more bullshit." As though it suddenly occurred to him, he added, "And I'm not remotely gay."

"*That* I can believe." Brice harrumphed. "Fine. If you move here, or close, I'll be here too."

Brice was really surprised when Tucker truly relaxed for the first time since showing up the day before.

"Come on, you're here. I'm putting you to work." He stood and waited for his brother to join him. *Someone* was going to help him in the garden that weekend.

"Doing what?"

Brice didn't answer, just made sure Tucker followed. He held the rear door and heard, "Holy shit! Memaw really rubbed off on you, didn't she?"

Brice laughed, shoving Tucker into the sunlight.

* * * *

"So you're okay if I do this?" Jake watched for any sign of disapproval from across the table.

Rebecca slowly swallowed, giving it thought. "You really are going to go through with it, aren't you?"

"If he says yes, then, yes."

"Mom is going to go overboard. You know that, right?"

"Let me worry about her." He reached for his daughter's hand. "The question was are you okay with it?"

"Does he make you happy?" She practically pierced him with eyes that knew too much.

"Yes."

"Are you in love with him?"

Jake's lips twitched and he finally smiled, imagining Brice's expressive laugh, his sweet smile, and his warm arms. "Utterly sunk like the *Titanic*," he quipped.

She popped a bit of broccoli into her mouth, refusing to rush. Finally she put her fork down and clasped her hands over her plate. Jake was practically sweating she was being so silently stoic. Fear of hurting his daughter was becoming real.

What she felt, how she felt over these changes he'd been going through since the spring were important to him. He didn't want to hurt her, which was why he'd taken his time to go over all his plans, explain his intentions, and make sure she fully understood he wasn't changing anything other than his residence—he hoped. That still relied on Brice, but he refused to think negatively. For the first time, he was truly happy with another person. He wanted to pursue this to the end. And hoped it had a happy one.

"If you really feel this strongly about him, then don't let anyone, me or Mom, stand in your way." She shook her head when he went to speak and he slowly shut his yap. "I'm almost eighteen, and we've been good, happy. But you deserve to be happy for *you*.

Mom's going to flip, and personally, I'd love to be a fly on the wall." She gave a demonic grin. *Yeah, that's my baby girl,* he thought with a silent cheer. Sissy had always resented that Jake and Rebecca had clicked better, communicated better. If she'd done more than circled around her own life... But that wasn't Sissy. So she'd lost out on a lot of Rebecca's dreams. Jake had supported her all the way to choosing Stanford. "Besides," she added. "I really like Brice. You two, crazy as it sounds, *work*. Just leave the spare bed open. I will be home for holidays."

He scooped up her hand and gave her a strong squeeze. "You got it."

Chapter Twenty

Jake opened the door expecting a really cute blond, and felt his heart hit his ribs when he found Sissy. "What are you doing here?"

She tried for a smile, hesitant and supposedly befuddled. "I can't just stop to say hi?"

"No." He scowled. "Please leave."

"You're not inviting me in?" Brown eyes widened in feigned hurt.

"No."

"Wait." She sniffed, then shoved herself halfway through the door. "You made roast. For just you and Rebecca?"

"What I cooked is no concern of yours," he growled through a tight jaw. "Now, go!"

"Okay. So where is she?"

"Rebecca is at a friend's for the night." Sissy wouldn't have known that, but it really shouldn't have mattered. He rubbed burning eyeballs. Gouging them out seemed like a drastic measure, but it was an option.

"Okay, then. Your date. You are dating someone, aren't you? Where is she?" She wiggled into the house and short of throwing her out by her hair—which he could fully imagine—he didn't stop her. "I want to meet her."

"There is no one else here."

"Then she's coming?" She pranced toward the kitchen. "I can wait!" she called over a shoulder, the clack of sandals on tile grating on his last nerve. Tight, skinny jeans and a long shirt of something that was probably one of her micro-dresses. She tried for innocent, even with her clothing, but never quite pulled it off.

"Fuck me," Jake muttered. Not how he'd wanted tonight to start. "Can't she grow up?" Then as if all the gods known to history were out to laugh at him, Brice's car pulled into the driveway behind his.

For just a moment he dreamed of running out to his car, hopping in and doing the Thelma and Louise number. *Anywhere.* Sighing, he knew that wasn't the way to deal with this, which he hoped would be the final time it would ever be addressed. He honestly expected her to never speak to him again.

Was it wrong that he was hoping for that outcome?

"You okay?"

Jake blinked and focused on the wonderful man on the steps, studying him with concern. "Perfect now." He smiled and offered a hand. A tender kiss followed in greeting, then Jake brought him in and closed the door. "We're not alone."

"I thought Rebecca..."

Jake shook his head, unable to prevent the scowl.

"Oh," Brice groaned with annoyance.

"Tell me about it. Might as well get the worst of it over. I have plans for tonight." He nuzzled into Brice's jaw.

"I think I'm going to like these plans." Brice's sexy sigh shot heat through Jake's blood.

I'm really hoping so. He'd had this in the planning since the July Fourth cook-off. Now it was time to initiate *Win Brice.*

Brice placed his bag inside the door and Jake cupped his hand. They walked together for the kitchen.

"I hope you don't mind, I opened a bottle of..." She turned toward them, and her voice stuttered into silence.

Sissy took one look at them and dropped the glass in her hand. It shattered in a spray of shards and slivers.

"Sissy!"

"Who is he?" Her voice was shrill, more a shriek.

Jake squeezed Brice's hand, subliminally telling him to stay put. He went to the side closet to find the broom and dustpan. "This is Brice."

"Where is your date?" she demanded.

"Quit, Sissy! You are not going to pull your drama bullshit tonight." He smacked the door closed and returned to where the innocent wine glass had lost its life. "You have met my date. Get out."

"No! It's true?" She clutched the counter in a shaking hand. "You're dating... I can't say it."

Brice crossed his arms and tipped his chin to gaze at her through his lashes. Jake knew that look. *Let her have it, baby. Both barrels!*

"Can't say what, *Sissy*? Hello? Nice to meet you? Or did you miss that class on common courtesy?"

She glared at him, trying to stay prissy and proper when it was just as fake a show as all her temper tantrums. Jake began to calm down. It wouldn't be a cat fight, but he had absolute faith Brice would be able to handle her attitude. It would be her mistake to think he wasn't up to the battle.

Sissy narrowed her eyes at him. "Jake isn't gay." She sneered in Brice's direction. "Like you could do anything for him."

"Like you could?" he stated with cool deliberation. "And gay or not isn't your business."

"But Rebecca—"

That was as far as Jake was going to let her push. "Is fine with everything. Unlike some people in this room, she respects personal space and choice." He dumped the swept up glass and returned the broom to the closet. "Now, please leave. And next time, call. Do not just show up. You do not live here. This is not your house to barge into."

"You'll be hearing from my lawyer! I will not let you subject *my daughter* to more of this—"

Brice's slow, sarcastic hand clapping stopped her mid-rant. "Ovation quality. First, Rebecca is eighteen in exactly nine days. Yes, I do know. Second, hearing from a lawyer for what? You're trespassing. And you've been asked to leave. I'm a witness. We can call the police."

"You do *not* live here," she nearly shouted, condescendingly.

"Actually, I do. My clothing is here. I have permission to be here. Care to push your luck?" As unruffled as a cool lake. Jake could see why he was so respected to stand in front of a classroom. At that moment, he'd agree with any argument Brice used if it got rid of Sissy that much faster.

Fury almost burned her through the floor. She glared at them both. Her mouth popped open, but she was brought up short with a pointed hand from Jake directing her out of the house.

"Leave. Now."

She stormed past them with a clipped stride. Seconds later the front door slammed shut.

"Wow," Brice gasped.

Jake took one look at his stunned face, strode across the space between them and engulfed him in a strong embrace. "Wow, definitely." He tipped Brice's glasses to remove them. All he knew was they were on a flat surface when he let them go. With a single surging step, he pressed Brice into the wall behind his shoulder and kissed him. Conquered him. Thrust between his lips and adored him.

He knew perfectly well why Sissy was being such a bitch. She'd officially lost Jake, and even though she'd been with who knew how many guys, so long as Jake was single and in the wings, she'd always felt superior. He was gleefully ecstatic to finally pull that rug out from under her.

Tunneling fingers into light blond hair, Jake lost himself completely in Brice's arms. The kiss could have lasted forever and he wouldn't have complained one syllable. He couldn't get enough of Brice's kisses. Jake muscled a thigh between Brice's legs and pinned him firmly to the wall, riding up and down against his crotch. Brice began to gasp and whine.

Fingers clawed into Jake's arms. Brice's spine arched. Jake gripped a hip and hiked him closer, lifting him off the floor into his pelvis.

"Drive me wild," he managed when he broke away for a much needed lungful of air. He loved the feel of Brice's weight, loved the taste of his skin, loved the heat of his kiss. Trying to remember how long he had left on dinner, he decided he'd much rather feast on Brice. "Do you care if dinner is late?"

Brice gulped then quickly shook his head.

Jake really couldn't help himself. He missed Brice so much during the week. He clasped one side of Brice's ass, grinding them together. The sucked moan from the other man drove him insane.

"You sound so good. So sexy," Jake told him, encouraging him.

Brice's head was thrown back, his mouth open as he panted, soft growls and whines slipping from between them. Like he was lost, drowning under Jake's passion. Somehow, Jake was going to convince him that he wanted the rest of their lives to give him exactly that feeling. Sissy's arrival had shoved a wrench into his initial plans, but he was used to working with what he'd been dealt when things went awry.

Catching his breath, Brice straightened and gripped at Jake's hair, pinning him in place then he homed in and recaptured his kiss, dueling with fevered intent, tongue to tongue. Jake felt himself melting beneath the returned volley of Brice's ardor. He'd rarely known a woman to challenge him. Rarely known a woman who'd wanted to take the upper hand. It was refreshing with a truly erotic rush to know that Brice could do that and liked to do it. It actually lifted a weight from Jake's shoulders. He *could* give Brice the reins and let himself go, let himself be taken rather than be the driver. He couldn't help but be intrigued by the idea. Even more, he was flattered that Brice liked him enough, wanted him enough to do it, to make him feel that good.

Hands moved of their own accord, gliding beneath shirts, tugging them free to whip over heads. Bare chest to bare chest. There was nothing to stop them as they both dove for pants waists and zippers. Neither could get naked fast enough. Shoes were kicked off. Clothes melted to expose aroused skin.

Jake roamed hungry hands across shoulders, down Brice's body, adoring, cherishing.

He hefted Brice and spun, setting him without apology on the dining table. He doubted they'd see dinner tonight. It really wasn't a concern at the moment.

Brice wrapped lean muscled legs around his waist and drew him close. Like he hated the thought of letting more than a few inches come between them, and even that could be argued.

He grasped at Brice and kissed him again, hard, staking a claim. Brice's throaty moans were adding fuel to the fire.

Jake slipped free to stand in front of him, panting, staring into Brice's eyes. "Don't want to let go," he murmured. But...he knew he had to. He needed the supplies in the bedroom. And he hated that fact, that he'd have to stop for such a simple yet important need. "How do we get rid of the condoms?" he asked. Jake had never really enjoyed sex with them, and knew there had to be a way to remove them from the equation.

Brice blinked. "You're serious?"

"Very." Though he hoped after this weekend, Brice realized *just* how serious he was.

"Blood tests," Brice answered in shock, as though he hadn't believed Jake had meant it the first time he'd mentioned it. "I will tell you this." He cupped a hand over Jake's mouth, keeping him quiet. "The only way I'll agree is as a committed partner. So think on it hard before you make that decision. I don't want you to regret it if you find a woman you want more."

Jake moved his hand away slowly. "You really think I'd want a woman more?"

"Jake." Brice braced his frame with a palm on the table. "All I want is you to be certain. I've never made the offer to be in a committed relationship, or accepted. It means that much to me that I want you to be the only one, but you have to be sure." He shot Jake an imploring look. "Understand?"

Something that had been screwing itself tight as Brice had spoken released with a whoosh inside Jake's chest as he grasped, he hoped, what was actually being said.

"Yeah, I think I do," he replied. Gently, he tugged Brice to him, curling arms around his shoulders to hold him close.

And honestly, realizing what Brice had just admitted made him love the man even more. Now Jake just had to convince him he meant it as well.

Right after he turned off the timer on the oven.

Chapter Twenty-One

Brice snagged on Jake's dejected, perturbed gaze and tried to hold in his laugh by pinching his lips, but couldn't, and soon both were chuckling roughly at their situation, echoed by the buzzing alert that dinner was ready.

Bare-naked on the table, and obviously interrupting something Jake had tried to do for an intimate meal for the both of them.

"I really need better timing for these moments," Jake groused. He sank forward to rest his forehead on Brice's shoulder, rocking both in joined humor.

"Will it hold for half an hour?" Brice curled fingers around his very stiff shaft and stroked it. It showed no signs of flagging. "I have a problem that you really need to take care of."

Jake murmured with hungry appreciation, his unblinking eyes trained downward on Brice's actions.

"Just... Just hold that...thought," he managed.

Jake slid away from Brice. By his distracted attention glued on Brice, there was no doubt it was reluctantly. Each step was staggered, stuttered and tripped. He watched Brice's motions with wide, deep blue eyes, hunger making them darker every second.

A couple blind jabs at the oven panel and the timer was silenced. Then Jake was right where he'd been in front of Brice, kissing him like Jake couldn't get enough of Brice's lips.

Palms and fingers splayed and kneaded across Brice's back, creating chills in waves to roll down his spine. Brice furrowed fingers into Jake's hair and held him, arching and tipping to deepen the kiss, to touch more skin. The hair on Jake's chest drove him nuts. Brice loved that Jake had waxed his sac and around his groin, but don't touch the chest! Frissons of heat erupted as they rubbed together, driving more blood through his body, surges that made him feel on fire and hardened his length until it strained against the frame leaning into him. Like the interruptions had never happened.

Jake tore his mouth away and shifted to glide down the column of Brice's throat. Goose bumps exploded along his arms as Jake swirled and sucked. As he felt the heat of building pressure, he knew Jake would quit before he left a bruise. The fact that he was conscious of that fact turned on Brice more.

Only this time, when Jake went to release him, Brice held him in place. "Do it," he growled. There were weeks of summer left to let it fade. And right then, he wanted it. He wanted to carry Jake's mark. *Fuck you, Sissy. This man is mine!*

There was a split second, a questioning hesitation, then it was like Jake wanted to try his best vampire imitation right there in his kitchen. Brice cried out with a harsh gasp, his eyes smacking shut as delicious pain burned him with arousal. Tipping his head, he stretched out the length of his throat, relishing the pressure. Jake trembled with the force of his hold, keeping Brice secure and steady. Brice pinned Jake's hips between his thighs, holding him as ragged pants rocked them both. Shudders of delight were growing. He hooked his feet behind Jake and all but curled around his body. Moans vibrated skin. Brice clawed at Jake's shoulders and back.

Brice was almost dizzy when Jake finally released him, licking over the spot with caring tenderness. "That's going to last a while, baby," he warned, sounding husky. "Looks as good as I'd imagined." Emotions flared like comets in blue eyes when they rose to Brice's. "Hang on."

Brice clutched tightly and Jake cupped his ass, pinning him to his chest.

"You're insane!" Brice cried when Jake tested his hold. He was really going to do this!

"Yeah, but you already knew that," he joked, lifting him smoothly off the table and turning to carry him to the bedroom.

Brice locked his ankles around Jake's waist. Hearts pounded. Jake's rapid pulse thundered against the press of ribs. He couldn't tear himself from Jake's stare.

Tenderly, Jake lowered him to the bed. Brice relaxed and Jake stretched out with him, covering him from shoulder to shin. Jake's kiss was one of the sweetest he'd ever known. Slow and seductive, it reawakened the heated desire they'd shared in the kitchen—the one that had them clawing at clothes like animals.

Jake wasn't shy in any way now, delving and stroking, licking with his tongue to lips and within. He traced the roof of his mouth, then dueled, teasing him into quaking whimpers. Brice snagged at him and suckled when he caught his breath. Jake groaned, lashes lowering as sensation shot through him. There wasn't any part of the male anatomy that Jake avoided. Brice hissed as he slithered down his chest, licking and nibbling at pressure points and dips.

The gentlest pressure of a kiss to his scar careened a shiver up his frame. Fingers gripped at Jake's shoulder and kneaded in answer. It was almost like Jake was blessing him, like he was more than grateful that Brice was still there when he did that. It was one of the reasons he adored the man currently ravaging him.

Jake moved further down his body, suckling little love bites, or licking just to make him moan. Warm breath enveloped his shaft then Jake took him into his mouth. Lava raged at Brice's core. A wave of heat rolled over him, tightening skin as he sought more of the unbelievable torture.

"Aaaaah," he gasped. "Love...yes." Brice couldn't think, and speaking was a fading possibility.

A firm palm cupped his balls right when Jake took him between his lips. It didn't matter that he couldn't take Brice deep. What he did with his tongue should have been labeled a secret weapon.

Pressure neared his entrance and Brice relaxed, giving himself over to Jake's exploration and shared pleasure. He didn't even know when Jake had found it, but the press deepened with added lube, gliding sinfully over skin that trembled in need. Brice furrowed fingers into Jake's hair, just wanting to touch as Jake split him apart. He lavished Brice's cock with hard and slow sucks to deep tissue licks that drove him up a wall. The occasional chuckle from Jake vibrated his spine, proving he knew how slowly he was winding Brice up.

"Jake," he whimpered. "Please."

Muscles flexed as the heat and pressed tension of fingers vanished. Brice couldn't find him with his fingers. He slid his eyes to half-mast, searching.

"Open up, baby," Jake encouraged, kneeling, waiting.

He covered himself as Brice did, so hungry for what Jake was going to give him. So in need to come. Jake moved forward and tugged Brice closer at the same time. The slick push breached him, and Brice arched his neck pressing into the pillows as his body accepted and stretched. "Oh, fuck...fuck. Yes!"

"Never heard a sweet teacher cuss like you do."

"All man in bed," he returned between jagged breaths.

"Very...glad...of...that," Jake bit out between rigid pumps.

Brice's body rolled in answer and met Jake's hips, the press of flesh warm outside, scorching him inside. Then Jake moved, urging Brice to bend and flex and with a wriggle, Jake lay on his back with Brice staring down at him, deliciously impaled.

"Ah hell." Jake ground his teeth. "So fucking good." Blue eyes glistened and sparkled like ice staring up at Brice.

Brice shifted his weight and both gasped. Jake fit him perfectly, hitting every nerve up to Brice's throat. He began to move and Jake guided him, strong hands on his hips. Neither closed their eyes, staring into unblinking windows, darkened with untapped desires. Sparks sizzled over nerves with every movement.

"Harder, baby. Please," Jake whined, pitching his hips, urging for more.

Brice leaned back, bracing his hands and rode Jake like a pro bull rider. Jake shook and trembled.

"*Fuuuuuck!*" he screamed, his spine bending and snapping. "Right...there!" Jake's dick throbbed within Brice's channel. Skin began to glisten as surges of desire flooded veins.

Brice had Jake at his mercy. He panted Jake's name. "Me," he pleaded. "So good." Drips were flowing from the end of his cock, hitting flesh with each pop of his dick as he bounced. Each racing heartbeat forced more against already swollen skin until he ached with the need for release.

Jake's hand was firm and harsh, gripping and tugging, jerking him off as they both soared to the top of the clouds. It took next to nothing for Brice to unload, streams of spunk lining Jake's abdomen while he filled Brice's ass with deep thrusts. Then Jake stiffened and heat touched him from the inside out as he jetted into the condom.

Gray warped his vision as he sucked air, floating forward, his spine melted. It was probably all the liquid on Jake's chest. He managed gulped breaths unable to move a muscle, molding himself into a firm shoulder and corralled by caring arms.

I love you so much. He really wanted to say those words but managed to swallow them at the last possible second instead. Jake had come a long way since their first kiss. Brice believed he wanted to make this work, but... And that was the issue. That *but* in the middle of everything.

Jake had been married. Brice didn't hold that against him. What worried him, in a nutshell—was other women. If Jake decided he wasn't ready to give that up in his life, if a woman drew his attention, Brice would be devastated. It was an underlying fear. One he'd already suffered from every member of his family. He knew what it felt like to be pushed away, to be looked at like he was less than the rest. To not be enough.

To be severed from every family member he'd known, and called dead.

His chest shuddered as his emotions swung wildly.

Jake's family wasn't an issue. Not with Caleb and Ian, not with their hodge-podge group of friends.

Brice didn't have any family to worry about. Well, now Tucker, but if he didn't like it, tough shit. He believed his brother was coming around. He was convinced it was more than just seeing people like him in real time. He probably had made friends through work that were gay. Knew people. Either way, it didn't matter to Brice.

Jake nudged him and they rolled to their shoulders on the bed. Brice whined as the fullness he'd experienced faded and slipped away.

Lingering kisses brushed over his lips. Brice arched on his neck for more of them. This right here was one of the reasons he held hope that he was more important than an experiment, that Jake wouldn't look at another woman. No lover, no boyfriend, had ever been this attentive, this caring. Like everything he was doing was with his whole heart. From the weekend when Brice had needed the helping hand to every moment they'd spent together since. Jake treated him like Brice was his whole world.

He only wished he could trust it.

Brice closed his eyes as the kisses continued, hiding his thoughts from the man adoring him.

He was drifting beneath those kisses when Jake told him, "Let's take a quick shower and go eat."

"Hopefully it's not ruined," Brice said, burrowing under Jake's chin. It was too tempting to reach out and lick with the tip of his tongue as close as they were. Jake's chest shivered in answer to the teasing flicks.

The unhurried press of a hand beneath his jaw raised him. "Even if it is, nothing is as important as you."

The intensity was maddening. Rolling them again, skin to skin, Jake hung above him.

Brice swallowed. His heart tripped.

"No interruptions this time," Jake said. "I wanted this weekend to be perfect."

"It already is."

The smile Brice received was beautiful. The kiss they shared was merely icing on their cake.

Chapter Twenty-Two

"You never did say why Tucker was in town, or what happened between you two." Jake finished loading the dishwasher while Brice straightened the table.

"My father died in February. He's the only reason I would have ever known."

Jake straightened to gape at Brice. "They really disowned you? Completely out of the family?" Jake had known what had happened between Brice and his family, but this was even more than he could fathom. To not let him know his own father had passed? It was inconceivable on so many levels for him.

"From everyone in my family, to cousins, aunts, uncles, friends of the family." He shrugged. "I wasn't going to beg to be where I wasn't wanted."

Jake reached for him, a hovering hand that trembled. Brice spied it and met him. Linking their fingers together, Jake urged him closer. "So Tucker..."

Brice folded into Jake's chest and Jake let him, curling arms around his waist to hold him close, as close as he wanted.

"Went against family, though I really don't know how many, if any, knows he's here. He said he'd been hunting for me for the last few years and that Mom refused to give him any help or information. That's not all that surprising. She probably burned everything with my name on it, junk mail or otherwise. Can't have the dead reappear, even if it's only a label on a flier."

"What's he planning on doing?"

"Staying close. He wants to break from the family, but on his terms. They've really put a lot of pressure on him to remarry and after his first, he just can't do it right now."

"Wow. He was married?"

Brice chuckled a little rudely. "He's not all that bad. At least, not usually." He leaned to peek at Jake. "Besides, your brothers aren't exactly perfect."

Jake snorted. "Uh, no. Point made. Will he be staying with you?"

"No. I'd kill him. Or *vice versa*. He said he found a cheap place to live while he was looking for work. He's a construction guy to the bone. Good with wood, though. Carpentry," Brice added when Jake coughed to hide his initial reaction.

"Yeah. Yeah, sure," he rattled off quickly. But that alleviated one worry. Tucker *would not* be staying with Brice. "Are you okay now? About your father?"

Brice hiked a shoulder, not retreating further. "As much as I can be. I hadn't really thought about any of them in a long time. It was just a hard shock. First seeing Tucker, and then being told that."

Jake rubbed his back. He could imagine and doubted he came close to what Brice had suffered. "Are you going back?"

"No."

Jake hadn't realized he'd tensed initially with the question until he went slack with a quiet exhaled whoosh. He tucked Brice up close. He really had planned out the whole weekend but since the moment he'd opened that door and found Sissy, he should have known things weren't going to be that simple. At least now with those wrinkles out in the open and cleared, he could move forward.

"Remember when I said I had things to do here at home?"

Jake nodded.

"Well, Rebecca is on course to enter Stanford in about six weeks." She almost tore down the house with her screams when she received the acceptance letter.

Brice leaned out of Jake's embrace and blinked at him questioningly. "She's in?"

"With flying colors."

Brice beamed. "Bet you're proud."

Jake really was. She'd been working hard to go there since her eighth grade year. She had set her sights high and had never let her aim falter. Jake knew what that took to accomplish.

"But that leads me to what comes next."

"Oh?"

"And it depends on you."

"Double oh?"

That made Jake smile. "Yes." He looked around the room, a rueful twitch to his lips. "Although I hadn't expected it to happen in the kitchen."

"What?"

"Well..." Jake slid out of his arms and reached for a hand, twitching gently when he had it. "First, I was going to lure you into the bedroom—"

"Which you already did," Brice pointed out playfully.

"Which I already did," Jake agreed, not at all sorry for that divergence. "So I guess I have to go with Plan B." He started to walk backward for the living room. "Something you said earlier was actually key in this weekend's success."

"Okay, now you have me saying more than oh. What are you doing?" Brice asked, smiling in confusion at his teasing and evasion.

"Well..." Jake urged him to sit on the couch, sitting with him. "This is part of it." He handed several face down pages to him to read.

Brice shifted through the pages, one after another. "You're selling the house?" Confusion twisted Brice's brow.

"I am, but..." He wiped his hand over his knee, trying to calm his nerves. "Only if you say yes."

"If I say yes? Why would what I say matter to you selling the house? Where are you going?"

"I'm hoping with you," he admitted.

"With me?" he breathed in surprise.

He slid the pages out of Brice's fingers to capture his hands. "I want to really try this Brice. I want to try with you."

"Try?" Brice swallowed hard. Green eyes were wide like pools of moss behind thin glasses. "Like an experiment?"

"No. *Try*. As in, try to make it permanent. I've made arrangements to move my work to Jasper. I can by the end of summer, once Rebecca is in her dorm." Jake was fighting to gauge Brice's reactions, his silence, and couldn't.

"You want to move in...with me?"

Okay, that was definitely shock and disbelief.

"I want to be *with* you," he corrected. "I think you're missing the bigger picture." Going for broke, and figuring his next move would make the largest impact, he slid from the couch and rested on a knee in front of him.

Brice's jaw slowly unhinged.

Doing what he'd always done, he wriggled fingers into his until they threaded neatly together. "This is what I mean, baby. With you. Together." The silence in the room lengthened. "Brice?"

Jake had hoped there'd be a little more joy, maybe even *happy* surprise, not this quiet debating that was making his stomach churn. "Talk to me," he urged.

"I... I don't know what to say," Brice replied, subdued.

"Say yes!" Jake tightened fingers, bringing that captured hand to his lips. "You know I care for you."

"I do," he whispered.

Slowly he lifted his chin from where he'd dropped to stare at their joined hands. The hollowness in Brice's eyes almost killed Jake on the spot. "You don't." He said it bluntly, starting to see where he'd taken the wrong turn. He was invested. Brice was not.

Brice swallowed. Hard. "I do, Jake." He wet his lips and took a very slow breath. "I love you."

The freefall of his heart ceased, climbing out of his gut in slow, cautious increments with those three little words. "You love me?"

A firm squeeze on his fingers seemed to be the only confirmation he was going to get at that moment.

"But you don't want to be with me. Is that it?" Jake didn't know what to make of Brice's withdrawn silence.

"I do, so much," he choked out. Blond lashes fluttered, hiding eyes that were starting to glisten. "But..." He faded into a thick silence. "But if you found a woman, someone better—"

Jake leaned forward and kissed him hard, caught between a shout of victory and one of anger. Jake palmed the back of his head and kissed him until Brice went limp. He kneaded at skin and bit at lips until Brice relented. Until he opened up and met his challenge.

Panting, Jake released him with just enough space to speak. "Listen to me. If I had wanted a woman I would have found one. Do you really think in the last nine years, I didn't have the opportunity?" He tried to keep himself from rambling, but the words tumbled out of his mouth without regard to his wishes. "I wasn't looking," he stressed. "For a woman, or honestly, a man." He slowed, relaxing a hair when Brice's tension began to fade as he listened. "Let me tell you what changed that."

Carefully, Brice nodded, willing at least, and not running.

"Caleb's wedding. You were smiling and I couldn't stop staring. Here's all these guys built like bulldozers, and there's this one guy with the sweetest smile I could ever remember. He smiled with his whole being. His mouth." Jake danced a light thumb over his bottom lip. "His eyes." Tenderly, he removed Brice's glasses to brush butterfly kisses to his lids. "Everything," he managed, almost choking up. He would never forget those first moments when meeting Brice changed everything and reawakened something within that had been long denied and unknowingly left hungry.

Returning Brice's glasses, he added, "And then that same wonderfully sweet man shocked the shit out of me. He was intelligent, brilliant really, caring, and patient. And I was grateful to call him friend."

Warmth bled into Brice's cheeks.

"But it was more than that. He was all the things I would have expected in an intimate partner. I started falling for him."

Brice's lips parted with a gentle gasp.

"Yes, I love you too," Jake admitted, though as far as plans went, he was somewhere around L by now. "Will I find women attractive? Probably." Brice scowled and Jake smiled gently. "Will it matter? Not in the least. No more than other men would be for you, I hope. No one could know what would have happened if I'd never met you. Another woman? Maybe. Another man? Equally maybe. The thing is, you were the one I found. That is all that matters to me."

"It's hard," Brice offered, slanting a glance upward through damp and spiky lashes. "I've already lost one family because I wasn't perfect enough."

"I know, baby. But we're your family now. You said it yourself. The whole town, really. Rebecca and I would like to be *your* family."

A shudder almost toppled Brice, but Jake held him steady.

"Both of you?"

"She adores you." He kneaded blond hair and skin again. "And I love you. I thought on this and realized realistically, I would have to come to you. I want to."

"You do?"

Angling, he tapped the realtor pages on the table at his side where he still knelt. "Is that convincing enough? All I have to do is sign on the dotted line and fax them on Monday." He clasped both of Brice's hands. "Now, I'm asking again. Will you try with me?"

After a silence that was making Jake dread the answer, he finally heard, "Yes." Jake squeezed his hands, bringing Brice's focus up. It was a leap for Brice. He knew that. Yet nothing felt better, or went deeper than the flare of wanting and happiness that was starting to break through the clouds of his doubts. He wanted Brice to feel secure, to know Jake meant what he was saying. He wasn't the type to create a relationship at the change of the season, like Sissy. He was the type who had always wanted a strong relationship. This time, he was convinced he'd found it.

Assured he wasn't going to collapse in relief—at least right at that moment—Jake kissed Brice, a sweet, slow promise. As one, they melted together to lie on the couch, Brice's warm body draped over his with loving hands cradling him.

A little later, Brice asked, "End of summer, huh?"

"Roughly." Jake curled an arm over Brice's shoulders. They lay entwined on the couch in contented relaxation. "I don't know how long it will take to sell the house, and I want her settled at Stanford before that happens."

Brice sniffed in forlorn playfulness. "I guess I can wait that long."

A quiet rumbled laugh slipped from Jake. He understood the sentiment. A future measured in weeks felt interminable.

Epilogue

"Is that everything?" Jake dropped the last box on Rebecca's small twin bed.

"I think so." She sank down beside the loaded box. "Wow. I'm really here." She gazed around the small space with an awed and dazed expression.

"Just promise me you will try to put your studies first. This isn't a community college."

She raised her right hand, groaning mildly. "I solemnly swear."

Brice caught Jake's eye as he swallowed. The conversation they'd had the night before they'd hit the road to drive Rebecca and her belongings to California was still fresh in his mind. Jake's baby girl was growing up, moving out and moving up. He was beyond proud of her. Except Brice didn't think it would hit him this hard. She wasn't his daughter, but he discovered how much he did care just the same watching her take the next step.

"Once you're settled, we'll get your holiday time scheduled and a plane ticket home."

She smiled for her dad. "Thanks."

"Excuse me," a quiet voice said at Brice's shoulder.

He inched out of the way, allowing a young lady to enter the room. The bustle of people, boxes, shouts and hollers was loud right behind him as others gathered in the dormitory hallway, either moving in, or helping. Or like many, just getting in the way.

"Rebecca?"

"Laurie?"

They smiled at each other.

"Did you need any help?" Jake offered the young girl as she plopped a large crate of items on her bunk.

"No. My brother is bringing in the rest."

Jake put an arm around Rebecca's shoulders. "Call the hotel if you need anything before we leave on Sunday." They were going to spend a couple of days there for themselves before driving back to Iowa.

"I will."

Brice swallowed, shocked at how close he was to tears himself.

"Is this your dad?" Laurie asked with a shy smile.

"Both my dads," Rebecca said without missing a beat. "Jake and Brice."

"Wow!" Laurie blinked then grinned. She offered a hand to Jake, who shook kindly. "Nice to meet you. My brother is gay so I wanted a roommate who understood."

"Not a problem." Jake's warm voice was like honey.

A tap on Brice's shoulder had him facing Laurie's brother. "Sorry." Brice edged out of the way to let him into the now quickly crowding room.

Jake stood. "I should probably go so you two can get to know each other and set up your room. Nice meeting you, Laurie."

Jake stopped right outside the dorm door and hugged Rebecca.

"You will call when you get home, right?" she told him.

"I will. Don't forget the phone works in two directions."

She rolled her eyes. "And I promise to stay out of trouble."

"Somehow I think our definitions of trouble are going to vary greatly."

She smiled, though it wobbled. They shared a strong hug and he let her go. Brice was almost knocked off his feet when she tackled him for a goodbye hug as well.

"Take good care of him, Brice."

"I promise," he whispered. "I love you both."

She sighed and relaxed, hugging him in goodbye. He pushed her hair away from her eyes and smiled.

Yes, he loved them both. Very much. His family.

About the Author

Diana DeRicci is the sexy, flirty pen name of Diana Castilleja. A romance author at heart, DeRicci's writing takes you into a saucier spectrum of sensuality and sexual adventure, where a happily-ever-after is still the key to any story. Diana lives in central Texas with her husband, one son, and a feisty little Chihuahua named Rascal. You can catch the latest news on all of Diana DeRicci's writing and books on her website listed below. Feel free to drop Diana an e-mail. She'd love to hear from you.

Visit her online at:
www.DianaDeRicci.com

PURPLE SWORD PUBLICATIONS
www.purplesword.com